Motel Girl

Stories by

Greg Sanders

Thank you for letting
us smash your piano.

With love & kisses,
Gregory Brett Sanders
8/16/08

RED HEN PRESS | *Los Angeles, California*

Motel Girl

Book design by Mark E. Cull
Cover design by Greg Sanders
Arrangement by Ben Mesirow

ISBN: 978-1-59709-111-4
Library of Congress Catalog Card Number: 2007943501

The City of Los Angeles Department of Cultural Affairs, Los Angeles County Arts Commission, California Arts Council and the National Endowment for the Arts partially support Red Hen Press.

Published by Red Hen Press

First Edition

Acknowledgements

Some of the stories in this collection appeared in the following publications, to which the author extends his thanks: "American Hoverfly" in *Essays & Fictions*; "Garage Door" and "Mr. Hallucinosis" in *Mississippi Review*; "Motel Girl" in *Blue Cathedral*; "The Sculptor" and "Lemon" in *Time Out Neonlit*; "Choco" in *Pindeldyboz*; "Port Authority (Part I)" in *LIT*; "PS2 Mouse Adapter" in *Opium Magazine*; "The Cure" in *3:AM Magazine*; "The Gallery" in *The Crucifix Is Down*; "L." in *Epiphany Magazine*; "Grey" in *The River Reporter Literary Gazette*; "The Seep" in *WV Magazine;* "I Am an Actuary" in *Pink Cadillac.*

For my parents—who gave me freedom.

CONTENTS

Choco

He spent twenty-two years in the Moscow Circus, part of a troupe of dancing bears. When at last he no longer wished to perform for children, to walk on his hind legs like an absurd biped, he revolted and was put up for adoption. I was twenty-eight when I took him in. I had no children and no husband and thought, let me see if I can do some good in this world. As one of the smaller bears, he was considered manageable and so adoption, rather than being sent to a zoo, was feasible. The agent in charge of finding homes for these retirees assured me that "circus fatigue" was common among dancing bears and should not be taken as a sign of the animal's impertinence.

As a freelance translator, I am often hired by the circus to accompany foreign schoolchildren during their visit to the ring. It was in this capacity that I had come to observe the bear regularly, and watched as he gradually lost his focus. He would drift away from the other dancing bears, ignoring the trainer's long stick, or he would butt another bear, knocking over the troupe like dominoes, making the audience laugh, but not his keepers. He was done for. The circus paid me a small stipend for his upkeep. They'd named him Choco for the rich, deep-brown color of his coat.

You develop a keen sense of hearing when you walk with a bear in Moscow. People whisper, "filthy beast," when they think they're out of earshot, even though I kept him very clean at first, shampooing him with scented soap from London. I wanted to be a good mamma, yet I was on a tight budget. My friend Aleksei and I would buy fruit from Moyerova, who had a kiosk on Tverskaya Street. Aleksei had a Soviet-era Geiger counter that he used to determine if produce was grown on the lovely green plains close to Chernobyl. If he got a reading, I would buy the fruit from the old lady for a few rubles less and then feed it to the bear. Though Aleksei sometimes objected to the practice, it did not seem to bother Choco. Being a bear, he remained as strong as one. For a time.

Choco was a small European brown bear, weighing no more than a human adolescent. If he pulled hard on his rope, it was usually because he spotted a small, brightly colored car that reminded him of the one he had been trained to follow around inside the circus ring. In that act, a clown would pop up out of the sunroof of the little car, see the bear trotting along behind him, feign befuddlement and terror, get back into the driver's seat and the car, with a few induced backfires, would be unable to accelerate out of the bear's range. Finally, the clown would get out and run off and Choco would get into the driver's seat, and by some circus magic, drive the vehicle out of the ring. The audience always erupted, sometimes giving a standing ovation. So, when he saw a brightly colored Mini or a Fiat 500, he would fall into his old role and attempt to run toward it with me in tow. When no one appeared out of the vehicle's roof, he would stop pulling on the rope and turn to me with a mystified gaze.

"My Dear Nadya," my brother wrote to me from Kyrgyzstan, where he was helping to negotiate a cap manufacturing deal for the Gap, Inc.

> You should meet a boy, and you won't do so with this bear attached to you. Will you give the bear a sense of independence so that you can leave it at home or send it out to the playground on its own? You must enjoy more freedom from your pet and find yourself a man. I have a friend, a

> painter, who loves animals. He says he is especially fond of bears. He saw you, sister, at the last New Year's Eve party at the Rutkoveski's. He was out by the woodshed smoking a cigar with his father. You went for a walk with the bear. They watched you under the moonlight. The father commented on your *pupechka*. His son commented on your long hair, which he said would be wonderful if not worn with such scorn, tightly bound above your pretty head. (And why, I must ask, were you not wearing a hat!) This was my first hint that the two of you might be a match. 'But the bear,' he asked, 'is she ever without it? It's such a curious way to live.'
>
> My friend's name is Vitaliy and when he came inside he said a few words to you and was prepared to ask about, and even caress, the bear, but he said you simply filled his glass with vodka and informed him that you must 'walk the animal,' even though you had just done so. Do you remember him? He embodies that rarest of contradictions—a man brutish in looks but gentle in nature. I am attaching his phone number herewith. Please consider calling him. He is handsome in his way, makes a good living *and*, as I said, is a skilled artistic person. I have also taken the unprecedented step of sending him your phone number without your approval. So if Vitaliy calls, do not be shy. At least let him speak to you?

But while my bear was identified as a distraction, as a usurper of my romantic energies, just the opposite was true. Without him I would have vanished years ago. I would have become invisible, as so many have in this city. My brother would not have written; his friend would have taken less notice, if any.

It was because of the animal that I had, for example, my friend Vadim, a cataract-inflicted veteran of The Great Patriotic War who had an ancient bear named Doda that was nearly as blind as he. We would meet in the park and Vadim would gum indecipherable words to me as our bears looked at each other like prisoners of war.

And there was, as I mentioned earlier, Geiger counter Aleksei, a classmate from my university years who was so shy as to be incapacitated. His eyes seemed always on the verge of tears. Broad menisci of liquid poised on his lower lids were ready to burst should anything at all go wrong. "I am allergic to life," he would say when someone wondered about the state of his eyes. He was diminutive, with a diminutive paunch, but otherwise well-built, like a gymnast who enjoys beer.

It would have been difficult for Aleksei to express his affection toward me if we did not have Choco between us. The animal was both a "distancing element" that made me approachable and a "recipient object" for his admiration and love of me. It was easier for Aleksei to gently groom the bear, to talk like a baby to the bear, to look deeply into the bear's large brown eyes than to do these things to me. But I understood his intent—even if he did not. Aleksei's caring for the bear as he would really like to care for me sometimes meant that he cared for the bear with more intensity than I did. If I had to choose one creature to live, I would have chosen Aleksei over the bear. But I often wondered—would Aleksei have chosen me or the bear? I once asked him this after we had been drinking. He hesitated, rubbing his moist eyes with the back of his little hands.

"Nadya," he said, "I cannot imagine one without the other."

One week after I received the letter from my brother, his friend Vitaliy called.

"You know I saw you only that one night at the party," he said, "yet I am still intrigued by certain aspects of you."

"Such as?" I asked.

"Your figure, for one," he said.

He went on a little too long, but I didn't mind hearing that voice come through the yellow telephone receiver. He spoke slowly, without much inflection, stumbling at times, but underneath it all he was self-assured.

Later that week he picked me up in his old Lada coupe and we went to his sister's for dinner. Afterward he took me to a fancy coffee shop that had just opened at the Bolshoi, and then I said I needed to get back to the bear.

"Always you and the bear," he said, placing a roughened hand over mine. His irises were an opaque green, like cold, plankton-rich waters. His pupils were very small, as if I were giving off a great amount of light. He drove me to my building without protest, though he was silent for many minutes. For this man, who seemed to have had no company for months on end, this silence was worse than pleading. Even after so short a time I had become accustomed to hearing his deep voice, to getting confused by his meandering speeches. It was as if he was used to talking excessively, yet only to himself. At last we arrived at my building.

I began to gather myself to exit, but as I watched his heavily ridged face sag with disappointment, I said, "Well, why don't you come inside with me? Meet the creature you have heard so much about."

When I opened the door to the bear's room, its resident came toward me. I patted it on the snout and it pretended to take a swipe at me.

"Sweet thing!" I said, so that Vitaliy could see there was no danger in it. "You sit here and watch the television," I said to him, "and I'll go take the beast for a quick walk. There is liquor over there."

When I came back he was relaxing in the chair with an empty glass and a bottle of vodka on the table in front of him. He was ugly, as my brother had promised, yet there was something exquisite in his bad looks, or in the way he managed them. He had given up. He could do nothing about them. But those oceanic eyes. You could swim through them like a whale and not be hungry for a long time. And nothing, absolutely nothing, was alarming about the rest of Vitaliy. He was tall and a little bony, but you could see from his complexion that the blood was getting around with vigor. He was as un-bearlike as you could get, which was a nice change.

I filled his glass with vodka and we shared it, then did it again. We watched a television show about caviar. We learned that beluga sturgeon can live one hundred years, grow to ten meters in length, and weigh 800 kilos. When the female is about twenty-years-old she starts producing the valuable roe. We were silenced by the image of a massive, primordial fish being clubbed into unconsciousness on the back of a trawler. In the next shot she was being slid down a chute into a small factory. This was the "processing plant." She was incised with a scimitar-like tool and two hands, reaching into her body, removed her egg sac intact. She was still alive, quivering, as the procedure was being performed, but she would soon die. Was such cruelty possible? I led Vitaliy into the bedroom.

When we were a little way into it the bear began to grunt in its room on the other side of the wall. I knew Vitaliy couldn't hear it, but I did, like a mother attuned to the nocturnal sounds of her infant. Then it began to knock against the wall in imitation of what it heard.

"Your friend," Vitaliy said.

"My friend," I said.

"He's jealous," Vitaliy said. I could hear its claws breaking through the plaster on its side, then pulling at the lath boards.

"This is unusual," I said.

"I can't concentrate anymore," he said at last. "Will you please do something?"

But suddenly the bear was silent, as if it knew we were no longer making love. Soon Vitaliy was ready again, but you can guess what happened when we started up. The bear would have none of it. It was no good. From then on we had to go to Vitaliy's place to make love.

He lived in a large loft of a warehouse where scenic backdrops of operatic and theatrical productions were painted. Vitaliy was regarded as a master of this art and was given his living space, gratis, by a consortium of theatre producers who admired him and depended upon his skill. In addition, he acted as a security guard for the entire warehouse—whose other vast rooms housed costumes, lighting equipment, props, and the machinery that made seas churn and singers levitate. He had a double bed and a washbasin, but to bathe properly he had to use the utility room in the basement where the artists cleaned their brushes and other tools of the trade.

Scenic panels were stacked two and three deep against the walls of his room: the Eiffel Mountains, medieval London, a frozen battlefield strewn with Napoleonic corpses, the Manhattan skyline, even a Martian landscape. His bed was in a corner of the room where he had placed two large panels from Denyevski's "Moonlit Moscow." Above his headboard St. Basil's cathedral gleamed with freshly fallen snow. A small moon, bearing herself with Russian humility, appeared in the top-left quartile, with fine clouds, like a silver gas, reflecting her light. It was Vitaliy's greatest piece, yet it did not carry his signature. Only individuals entrenched in theatrical arcana knew the name of its creator. When the great Belgian soprano, Edmée Bethean, performed her last aria, this very panel had been on CNN for all the world to see.

I began to spend more and more time with Vitaliy, keeping him company while he painted in the evenings. I did what I had to do for the bear, but its maintenance had now become a chore. We would still buy fruit at Moyerova's, still stop in the park to see Vadim and Doda when possible, but it was all rushed, disingenuous, on the clock. Now when small, brightly colored cars drove by I would simply tug on his rope and shout "No!" permitting the animal to relive not even one moment of its glory days. Before long, the poor beast began exhibiting lethargy; the cause of which I presumed was depression. I tried to alter my schedule and tend to him early in the morning if I knew I'd be with Vitaliy on that night. But more and more often it would be Vitaliy who, preferring me well-rested, would lift his long body out of our warm bed at six in the morning, drive to my flat, walk and feed the bear, and then return to me with the smell of the animal on his clothing. It was not a situation that could last. I had messages on my answering machine from Aleksei. He missed seeing the bear. When could he visit it? The creature had begun acting out in its room, defecating without schedule, and vomiting. On a clear Sunday afternoon in the park it even attempted to maul the harmless Doda.

★ ★ ★

One evening, when Vitaliy had a tight deadline and had to work through the night, I went home to sleep in my own bed. Late at night I was awakened. In the darkness I heard the bear whining as if it were having a nightmare, the strange, otherworldly grunts coming through the wall. On it went into the sunlit hours. In the morning I had a terrible thought and called Aleksei, telling him he must come over at once and to bring his Geiger counter.

He arrived, freshly showered and cologned, with an ivory-handled grooming brush to which he had tied a ribbon.

"I want to let the bear know I haven't forgotten him," he said, "even if others have forgotten me."

"Come and see your papa," I said to the bear.

He came slowly out of the dark room, dazed, his head hanging low and moving in little arcs. Bits of soiled newsprint from his bedding were stuck to his hindquarters.

"What *happened* to you?" Aleksei said, rubbing the animal's snout.

Vitaliy had planned to come by after presenting his latest panels to the consortium, and now he came through the door, paint-stained, spent, out of breath. I introduced the two men.

When Vitaliy went into the bathroom Aleksei pulled me aside and said, "You are dating a gorilla."

"I know," I said. I should have added that he was a gorilla with God's eyes and Michelangelo's hands.

Aleksei began examining the bear. "You see here?" he said, pointing to something behind the bear's ear. "There is a lump like a hockey puck. And look, he has a bald spot the shape of the Ukraine on his back. And here, a lesion. And his gums are bleeding. How could you not notice *any* of this?"

"Please take a reading," I said.

Aleksei took the Geiger counter from his canvas satchel and passed the sensor tube over the bear. The meter hopped. I thought of all those fruits and vegetables from the Ukraine, from Belarus, from the same poisoned soil to which a million children were slowly returning.

"He is dying," he said, "and it is poisonous for us to be around him. The cesium stays in his body. The little old fellow can't handle it any more. He is saturated. What did you expect?" He turned to me now with his little red lips. "And all to save a few rubles. Well, are you now rich?

"You two go back to wherever you've been all these months," he said, directing his attention to Vitaliy as well as me. "I'll stay with the bear. Leave a phone number, but go now."

We did as requested.

What horrors lurk within each of us, what black blood runs through our veins. Aleksei called about a week later.

"I don't know what came over me," he said. "I took him to my family's dacha intending to shoot him, but instead I hanged him from a tree. It took some work. I almost couldn't do it. Nadya, sweetness, forgive me. You know I did it because of you."

I said nothing.

"I called him by name, something you rarely honored him with. 'Choco,' I said, 'you are a wondrous beast. What happiness you have brought to all of us!' And then I hanged him. I pretended we were in the circus and I commanded him to stay stock still as I fixed the noose around him. It was like a miracle. What do you think of that?"

"I think you are a monster."

"No, it was very dignified. You could see in his eyes he was pleased to be so far from Moscow, from his life with you. If he could have, I am certain he would have frolicked up there in the forest, but of course he was a mess."

"You are not the Aleksei I've known for a decade," I said. "You are ill."

"Well, perhaps I too am suffering from radiation poisoning. I want to tell you that our Choco looked me in the eye and seemed to thank me. I felt a sharp dagger go deeply into my heart, but at least I felt *something*, you understand?"

★ ★ ★

I continue with my translation work and still lead French or British schoolchildren to the circus when the job calls for it. And in the evenings, after the other scenic artists leave, my gorilla boy and I bathe together in the large tub in the basement. Artists' imitations of crude graffiti cover the walls and the air is dangerous with the odor of solvents. If we feel it is safe, we light a kerosene lamp, undress before each other, and immerse ourselves in the tub. Buoyed, in the gangly embrace of my Vitaliy, I sometimes think of Choco in all his loping innocence, and each time I hope it will be the last vision of him. But I know he will be with me until my end.

American Hoverfly

Armine is remembering his last afternoon with Billi. He was under their favorite apple tree, lying on his back, looking up past the blossoms, past the honeybees that fed on their nectar, at a window of sky being bisected by a contrail. The jet was drawing its chalk-line through the center of the only patch of sky visible through all those branches. Billi stood over him and shook the branches so that apple petals rained down. She moved up and down on the balls of her bare feet. Her calves, which faced him, compressed and then elongated. She was laughing up there, her head hidden from view in the dense leaves of the bottom branches. She might have been laughing at him or she might have been thrilled with the whole damn scene.

"The bees are going to be very unhappy with you," he said.

"The bees can eat me," she said.

"They might do that."

Billi had taken to calling the tree Babushka. Shaped like an old lady who'd had a tough time, it grew out of a hillock and was bent in an arc of about fifteen degrees. The soil around its base was eroded, roots sticking out like bony elbows and shins.

On that afternoon other things were happening: goldenrod, globethistle, fiddlehead ferns were beginning to push up out of the meadow that surrounded the tree. And down below in the valley, in the couple's weekend bungalow, all those ladybugs had finished overwintering. The survivors were finally lifting their spotted elytra and unfurling their membranous wings and flying into walls like tiny, drunken biplanes. They had to be guided out, either through the porch door or an opened window. He and Billi had found the weightless corpses of the unsuccessful lodgers during the course of the winter—rolled up in the shades, under the dish-drying rack, in the light fixtures, dead on every window sill. And they'd seen the live ones crawling under the Mr. Coffee, lethargically moving up patches of sunlit wall, seeking any semblance of heat. He and Billi deposited the colorful, pill-like bodies of the dead ones in a jar they kept on the kitchen windowsill. From a distance it looked like a jar of candy. In drunken moments they planned an elaborate funeral pyre in the fireplace.

They'd shared a big mug of black tea with maple syrup and milk. Wild leeks they'd picked from the hillside and rinsed in the creek were drying on a dishtowel in the shade. That was it—that was precisely the setting. Under Babushka, the earth was cool and bare in spots. They'd done it here before, braced securely between sections of thick root, only this time Billi wasn't on the pill.

They liked to talk dirty—filthy, really—to each other while screwing. Usually. But the idea of going about their routine seemed like it would foul up the kid somehow—if she were to get pregnant this go around. Make it a pervert or malcontent. Sex under the banner of procreation is not at all the same beast as the porn-influenced screwing they'd grown accustomed to. So they were quiet now, and the sex seemed weirdly quaint, and Armine thought he ought to think tender thoughts to influence the outcome of the kid. But all he could think about was what a dirty fucking couple they'd become. That they were asking a lot of themselves. How could they be expected to switch gears so suddenly and create something tender, with tiny organs and limbs, and a cerebrum the size of a plum?

Armine kept his thoughts to himself and felt her bucking, and heard the animal slapping of their bodies against each other, and felt her short nails pinching his nipples. He looked at her fine body, honed by years of gentle exertion—yoga, rollerblading, swimming, sex, ultimate Frisbee. And the insects were making a racket, as if stimulated by the action, as if acting in inter-species concert, their feral shrilling rising up from the valley and descending from the tree tops, coming at them from every direction.

When he was about to come—and it had taken longer than usual—she grabbed his shoulders and began pushing him off. She looked terrified.

"Pull out," she whispered under her exertion.

"What?"

"Armine, pull *out*."

"I lost my nerve," she said afterward. "Something felt wrong. I don't know—*are* we ready?"

He turned toward her and cleared her bangs away from her eyes.

"We're not wed to this," he said. "I could've used a condom. Or, you know, we could have done other things."

His semen was settling into the stringy grass next to her and had pulled along loose grains of earth and a struggling katydid. She stood up, bent over, and kissed his forehead. He watched her get dressed.

"I'll want to hear about those other things in detail," she said, "but now I just need to get out of here. Maybe go for a walk or something."

Get out of where? he wanted to ask. Get out of the outdoors?

"Well then I'm gonna be a guy," he said, and began to doze off theatrically. She piled his clothing on top of him and disappeared over the ridge and down the wooded incline. A few minutes later, half asleep, he turned to see that an army of ants had surrounded his semen and were carrying off tiny globules of it.

When he came down to the house he saw her note on the fridge: "Went for swim, sleepy boy." It was late spring and not yet quite hot enough for most people to swim in a pond, but that was her style. She liked the invigoration, the shock of the water on her body, the bracing air, and it meant she'd probably have the pond to herself. It was a ten-minute walk. She'd take her usual quick dip, he figured. And, knowing her and her moods, she'd probably do it in the raw. He wasn't sure when she'd left, but he figured he had about an hour to kill.

He started to mow the lawn with the old two-stroke walk-behind that came with the cottage. It put out a huge cloud of oily smoke when he started it. Something about that he enjoyed. So much the opposite of how he'd been raised, with his parents getting the first electric mower on the block. Those old two-strokes, the puttering of the camshaftless engine, all the chrome-plating—he was pushing around nostalgia on wheels. A half hour passed before he came around to the stunted, shaded section of lawn behind the house under the firs. It was really just weeds, bedded pine needles and forget-me-nots. That part of the yard gradually sloped down to the edge of the creek where things became weedier still and where frogs often hung out on chic pieces of "uncut bluestone," for which city people were now paying through the nose.

He turned the mower off and took a look at the hill, and above, at the glowing fringe of the meadow in all its Universal Studios garishness. He could see the apple tree's crown of blossoms peeking over the ridge a little past that fringe. The sun was still high but it struck the young things growing up there—the saplings and tender grasses—at an oblique angle and lit them up with a green that seemed, paradoxically, unnatural. And the hill wept where springs broke through the rocky facade, marking their paths with algae and throwing tiny clouds of silt into the clear creek, like smoke. The late afternoon bugs were coming out, chirping, whirring, seeking mates.

Suddenly a small insect hovered in front of Armine's face, fixed in space as if frozen in time. The American hoverfly. He'd looked it up in *The Gardener's Guide to Bugs and Grubs* the previous summer. It had been rated with a "B" in a circle, for Beneficial to Gardeners. Its larvae eat aphids. That previous summer he'd also discovered a trick. When you saw one hanging in the air close by—and it seemed that's exactly what they liked to do—

you held your finger out as if you were pointing at it, and you sternly moved that finger close to it until you found that the American hoverfly was drawn irresistibly to your fingertip, like iron filings to a magnet. So that's what Armine did, lifting his finger, moving it toward the insect until the insect was locked into position. Under exactly what environmental pressures the insect had evolved this talent for hovering sarcastically so close to an object he could not imagine, but it surely had to do with eating or screwing.

As he wagged the finger, and then spelled his wife's name in the air with it, the hoverfly followed the motions precisely, as if attached by an invisible rod. It kept a fixed distance from his fingertip. Not one and a half inches or three inches but, Armine felt certain, a precise number of *insect* units of measure. Then, as if it had had enough of the game, it moved to hover beside his left ear. He could hear the zuzzing of its tiny wings. Was it trying to tell him something? And then it shot off into the torrent of the spring air like the world's smallest projectile.

He turned to see Billi standing in the front yard, among the tire tracks that crisscrossed the lawn. She'd been watching him. She held a fern in her hand. She'd probably dug it up from along the path to the pond. Its roots were heavy with soil, its fronds collapsed. She always found some shady spot on the property and replanted them. About half survived. He felt some affection in her now, from the way she looked at him as he walked toward her. The tilt of her head, the way she stood with one knee behind the other—girl-like and vulnerable; observant without being judgmental; Edie Brickell in that first video she did.

She wore loosely laced hiking boots on her sockless feet. He drew in a quick, shallow breath as if something were about to go wrong. As he got closer he could see she'd braided an aquatic plant or a cast of algae around her wrist like a bracelet. Her face shone with the sun she'd picked up these weekends in the country; it shone with the exertion of her swim and walk; it shone with everything that differentiated the two of them. She looked as if she wanted to say something to him. Something waiting in those dark irises of hers.

He heard a rumbling that got steadily louder until a Ford dualie flatbed laden with quarried bluestone worked slowly past the house, trailed by a cloud of rock dust and diesel exhaust. The driver downshifted as the truck hit the turn in the road past the house. It was on its way to the mill in East Branch, about ten miles farther on. When the quarrymen returned from their deliveries, the unladen trucks would speed past the house in the opposite direction, their leaf springs bowed and rigid, the trucks, celebratory, hopping over the smallest of bumps and sometimes shooting pebbles into the yard like BBs.

Billi used to cover her ears when they passed, more because she was offended at the quiet being shattered than to protect her hearing. He could see her think about it now, but he had told her a while ago that he thought it was offensive to the drivers, who were just trying to earn a living. So as the truck passed she kept her hands at her side and rolled her eyes instead.

Finally, silence fell on them again.

"I was hoping you'd come to the pond," she said. "You won't believe this. I was about to dive in when I heard this *snoring*. I looked across the pond and this man was on his back on that little muddy beach on the other side? His feet were in the water and his head was on the shore. I could barely make him out, but it was definitely a man and he was making quite a noise."

That little beach—Armine knew it well. An ancient water slide whose fiberglass tongue had delaminated long ago was sunk into the silt not ten feet from the shore. It looked like the kind of thing that would kill you if you tried to use it. They had no idea who owned that little beach and it always seemed draped in shadows and cloudy with gnats.

"He was really pale and I thought maybe he was dead. Except he was snoring, of course. I feel like we've seen him around."

"Where have we seen him?" Armine said.

"I don't know. It's just a feeling, like I said. But I don't have anything to back it up. Anyway, he must have been dead drunk. So, here's the thing. He was stark naked, not a stitch. I just stood there knee-deep in the pond watching him snore."

"I'll bet," Armine said.

"Should we see if he's still there? We should make sure he's okay. He could have, what you call it, inhaled his own vomit or something since I saw him."

"This is absurd," Armine said.

"What is?"

"Talking about our naked neighbor. Can you think of another topic? Anything more pressing?"

She was silent for a few seconds and shook her head as she watched any hope of levity vanish before her eyes. It was a beautiful day. Why did she always have to talk to him about so much *stuff*? It wasn't that she couldn't be completely open with him; it was that she was tired of *having* to be open with him at the drop of a hat. He'd always known that was a bad habit of his—the need for humorless meditation on any recent mishaps in their relationship. And her frontline weapon in these instances was sarcasm.

"Of course, honey. Let's talk about *us,*" she said. "Is that what you're getting at? You want to know why I asked you not to come inside me, don't you?"

"Now that you bring it up, you *commanded* me not to come inside of you."

"Like I said, I don't *know* why. Maybe nerves. Anyway, I don't want to talk about it now."

"That's pretty damn obvious. Did you come at least?"

"No," she said. "I did not come. Why do I have to come every time? And you should have asked me then."

"Did you want me to go down on you?"

"Enough already," she said.

He'd done it yet again, pointed out some petty violation of hers, brought it to a head, and then diffused it by changing the subject to something cute, as if the whole thing wasn't really worth worrying about in the first place. How she could have stood for it is a mystery to him.

"Please let's go to the pond and make sure that guy's not dead or something," she said.

They parked the Jeep in front of the path that led to the pond. Billi got out and lifted her foot onto the bumper to tighten her bootlaces, then the other foot. She never tightened the laces on one boot without doing the same on the other. It was always a matter of symmetry and evenhandedness with her, even when it came to inanimate objects.

Armine was already in the woods, on the path, watching her and waiting for her to finish with the laces, noticing, perhaps, the smooth musculature around her Achilles tendon where it emerged from the boot. As he likes to imagine it, he was about to tell her something—it's fine, let's not worry about kids or no kids and let's never again get into the nitty gritty of procreation.

But a truck, headed back to the quarry, empty of its load, celebratory, etc., came down the dirt road at full throttle. She never even finished tying her other boot.

* * *

The path is overgrown, barely passable, and splits a quarter mile from the road, one branch heading straight to the edge of the pond, the other, forking left, ending in a mossy clearing where a disused rowboat is chained to a hemlock. That's where Armine is now, hidden from view by a storm-felled honey locust, waiting for the ghost of his Billi. He'd heard from a neighbor that she'd been spotted here before, but couldn't get up the nerve to make a visit. But with the help of some Jack Daniel's and on the anniversary of her death, he's managed to give it a go. The only action on the pond so far involves dragonflies, which seem to be spending all their time mating in flight, tandem style.

But sure enough, after having perched for forty minutes in the shadows and drinking from a flask all that while, he sees her. She is not, as he'd both feared and hoped, naked. She wears that old orange bikini, its elastic frayed and its color bleached out from swims in chlorinated pools. She stands motionless a few feet from the shore. She is about twenty yards from him.

Oh god, he wants to shout her name, to hear her name echo through the valley. He also wants to know, should he have an erection? Because he does have one.

No wake spreads behind her as she moves forward. No concentric circles dissipate around her. Nothing. The surface of the water is so still that it's difficult to see where her body meets its reflection. The freckled cleft of her lower back is doubled below her and fades into the water.

From what he can tell at this distance, her gaze is fixed on a point across the pond. Then she turns to look around her. When her face sweeps his way, Armine's heart begins to beat so hard he can feel his mitral valve clicking. Prolapsing, the cardiologist calls it. He may be in actual danger if it doesn't subside. She turns her gaze back to the opposite shore and Armine follows it. He imagines the man she saw passed out there. Eugene Daigle—pink, cirrhotic, snoring.

The sight of that physique of hers: how he loved to lose himself in her. Why is there no fear in him? It is broad daylight. Might his neighbors—the Bosches, the Quinns, the Goulds—also be out here for the sighting, squinting through binoculars as he squats so idiotically under cover?

She immerses herself and sidestrokes toward the little beach with the old water slide. Then she stands in the water ten feet from the beach on which Eugene Daigle was once sprawled. Armine moves along the water's edge to get a better look at her. He enters a private yard—whose, he doesn't know—where he hears muffled news channel voices coming out of the woods. The United States is contemplating bombing Syria. He moves past the yard and into some brambles until he sees her clearly again. Her hair, flat and black against her shoulder blades, sheds no water.

"Hey," she says to the empty beach, not loudly. "Hey there, sir?"

It seems, he can't be sure, but it seems like she might be touching herself through her bathing suit.

She looks around again. She must have been considering whether or not to get out of the water and wake up Eugene Daigle. It would have been a hell of a vision for him to awaken to; her standing over him, dripping wet, and it would have saved her, too. But instead she swims back across the pond toward the path, getting smaller and smaller. She rises out of the water and fades into the woods at an altitude of about twenty feet. On ascending from the water, she seems not to exist below the knees.

Armine stares at the vacant beach, imagining Eugene Daigle waking up and meandering unevenly into the water up to his thighs, pissing and letting out a grand fart that he finds amusing (it makes a small ripple in the water). Then getting out, dressing, and leaving by a narrow path.

He had parked his flatbed a quarter mile away on an old logging road. According to his testimony, he passed out again in the cab and then, the sun getting low, tore ass to the quarry to pick up one last load of bluestone. That had been his intent, anyway.

⋆ ⋆ ⋆

Toward the end of that first summer after Billi died, Armine had regained his bearings and gone back up to the meadow for the first time since her death. It had been a dry August and the creek was low—a trickle. He climbed the hill and pushed his way through the tall, brittle grass to the old apple tree. Beneath it, between its roots, he believed he could still see evidence of having been there with Billi even though a few months had passed. Something about the way the ground was compressed and how the grass growing there looked different. And when he took a look at another spot a little farther away, a strange little plant was unfurling itself, neither fern nor reed nor sapling. Something dark-hued with an iridescent tint to its single curled leaf. He hadn't suspected it was anything special, just something new.

Mr. Hallucinosis

Jack X. stands on an aluminum ladder trying to find a joist in his ceiling so that he can install a thick steel hook and to that attach a looped cable into which he plans to slip his neck and hang himself. He's drilled several holes with a quarter inch diameter bit but has hit nothing but air on the other side of the plaster. You're beginning to get frustrated watching him.

For weeks you have been slinking around his apartment and your work is at last paying off. As he continues drilling, fine white powder drifts down and dusts the floor around you. You are hidden in the shadow of Jack X.'s chaise. It's ridiculous, you think, that a man who has set out to perform this simple task of carpentry at such an important juncture of his life seems so inept, so nervous. He drills more holes, quietly cursing his inability every time the cordless drill punches through the ceiling into nothingness.

After several more tries he hits a joist beneath the plaster, takes the threaded steel hook from a breast pocket, and screws it into the pilot hole. Wood shavings spiral to the floor. When he descends the ladder you take shelter properly beneath the chaise, not wanting to be seen before you are ready. You hear him gathering up the cable and threading it through the metal collar, a sound you've heard on a few other occasions.

Then he begins to undress—this desire to recreate one's state of arrival in this world when exiting it is standard—and you see that Mr. X. was once probably a good specimen, with a thick chest and muscled arms that have since gone flabby from all the drinking. He's wearing that mask that's part of the business, the expressionless joy of being in the last stretch, not at all a glorious joy, but then again not what his relatives will undoubtedly imagine—that he is weeping and fighting himself, under the influence of booze. No, he's miraculously sober and focused, a real go-getter. They're always so determined and at peace at this point in the process that it's as if they're running on some strange instinct, some primordial engine that once started cannot be turned off. He decides, last minute, to leave his briefs on, and for this you are grateful.

He ascends the ladder, slips the cable around his neck, and tightens it with a brief tug.

You run out onto the floor, shouting his name "Jack! Jack!" and waving your hands, somersaulting, touching yourself lewdly, laughing. At three inches tall there's no guarantee you'll be noticed at a time like this, but you think he sees you. He kicks the ladder out of the way on his first pendulous swing back. This kind of coordination in the throws of the act itself astounds you and you get on your knees and bow to him and his composure, as he swings above you, soon dead.

There was a time, and it wasn't that long ago, when your wife would accompany you on these gigs that you do, but she's recently taken ill, or so she says. You suspect she's having a bit of her own psychic break, what with all the misery you two catalysts of hysteria have instigated over the decades. She has lately become sympathetic toward your victims, as she calls them (you call them clients). You don't understand it. It's not why you were put on this earth, to sympathize with those whom you've come to push off the edge of sanity. This fellow, Jack X., your most recent, took weeks of hard work before he broke down, and you did it all on your own—no team work, no spousal synergy. What, then, are you supposed to do to get your partner, the love of your life, back onto the team? It's both a personal and professional dilemma.

★ ★ ★

A few months pass and you're in a log cabin surrounded by towering firs in the Maine woods. A fire is roaring in the hearth, spitting out popping, red-hot sparks. You are hiding in a pile of kindling in a wicker basket nearby. You have come in through the bottom of the basket where a hole, probably the purview of a mouse, provides a convenient means of egress. Again, you are alone, having left your significant other to her solipsistic moping, her creepy solitude. Next to you a beetle nibbles serenely at a bit of wood rot. It amuses you, the insect's banality, the lethargic, mechanical movement of its jaws.

Through the weaves of wicker you watch Suzanne, the young woman you've been working on in this bucolic setting. She is tied to a wooden chair, a Shaker number of some kind. Her wrists are abraded from struggling against the ropes, but she's calmed down now, exhausted, and possibly heading toward unconsciousness, maybe even shock. Milling about nervously is her lover, Janice, who seems to believe she is helping her sweetheart. Your existence depends on situations like this in which individuals disregard medical advice and go cold turkey without professional supervision. For days now Suzanne, who's volunteered to come here at the behest of her lover, has wanted a drink like somebody tossed from an airplane wants a parachute. Janice whispers to her, caressing her face. You can clearly hear encouraging phrases like, "Be strong, my beauty." This has been going on all day. She moistens Suzanne's lips and forehead with some cool water from an old dairy bucket, and she applies anti-bacterial ointment to the abrasions.

Things seem to be coming to a head and you're not sure you're making enough progress. Damn it, how you wish your wife were here. The theatrics you used to perform for your victims—screwing each other in plain sight, playing catch with a victim's possession, shouting into both ears as he or she is on the cusp of sleep. But now it's just you in this little cabin with these two not unattractive and, frankly, admirable women. Truth is you're envious of their devotion to each other.

It's not easy when there's a bystander involved. If she catches a glimpse, your life is most definitely over. Nobody's ever come back from that kind of exposure. Smashed with the heel of a foot and tossed into the white-hot coals—this is the fate you imagine for yourself should this clearly sober and solidly-built Janice, the exact opposite of her enfeebled and waifish lover, get a hold of you. You do not have the capacity to simply vanish and it's not like you have special transformative powers. And you're sure as hell not some giddy leprechaun, some amateur, feckless twit. You work hard, have a high success rate, and hope that when your career winds down you can spend your final years in Florida working on Alzheimer's victims at a leisurely pace. But now, alone in the midst of a state whose location is unclear to you, among the sort of women you grudgingly admire, you are almost ready to call it quits. The air of the cabin is suffused with the smell of these women, with the fire, and with the fir trees that are unfathomably tall. It would not, in the end, be so bad a place to end things. But of course you are not even close to throwing in the towel. It's not in your nature to give up, as they say.

When Janice leaves to use the outhouse, you're on. You walk slowly into the middle of the room and look up at Suzanne who, seeing you (a familiar sight by now), curses, then struggles with the ropes but can't break free. Her pupils are dilated and she's white with fear but at the same time hot and sweaty and struggling like a warrior to get free. She shouts, first softly, then hysterically. You moon her, wiggling your tiny, thumb-nail-sized ass at her for a few seconds. She shouts for Janice with all the fury her wracked body can muster. It's boring without your loved one here. You're bored out of your mind, but manage to run to and fro, whip around in circles, do cartwheels, flash her, et cetera. When you hear the door open, you sprint back to the basket, crawl in through the hole at the bottom, and take cover in the mess of kindling. You note that the beetle, the closest thing you have to a companion in this place, is still processing dead wood like a machine, unimpeded. It shows no sign of concern.

Janice, her belt still undone, holds her girl, rocking her back and forth. The fire is fading but the embers glow abundantly beneath the grate.

"In there. In *there*," Suzanne whimpers, pointing as best she can to the basket in which you are now suddenly alarmed.

Janice opens the basket and starts pulling wood out.

"There's nothing in here, baby," she says, continuing to dig down to prove her assertion. "Just some bugs."

The beetle, clinging to its shard blindly, flashes by you as it is lifted out. You suddenly are exposed and you see the shocked look on Janice's face.

You escape through the hole, running beneath Suzanne's chair and out the cabin door, which has been left open a crack. As you move rapidly through the underbrush you feel the thunderous stomping of Janice behind you. You remind yourself, again, while losing your breath, that none of your ilk has ever come back from being discovered. Panic remains at bay, on the cusp of glandular solidification. You wonder what it would be like to be held close to Janice's breast, to be crushed, slowly, excruciatingly, against her flesh. The woods stretch out vastly before you. You cannot even name the sort of animals that might lurk within this luxuriant habitat. If only your wife, your beloved, had been with you she might have advised you to be more vigilant, to pick a better place to hide, to refuse, as is almost never done, to even attend to this particular case. Why has she been so distant, so unable to accept her role? Might it be out of self-preservation? Could she have seen your fatigue, your small errors, your flawed judgment? Did she foresee your flailing strides through this underbrush? You cannot know for certain her reasons but you feel that though she is not with you physically, she shadows you spiritually. She is watching, her hands gripping one the other as tightly as a knot. In a day or maybe two, you are now certain, she will miss the sight of your little trousers hanging from their peg on the back of the bedroom door.

The sun is low. The forest floor is dappled with warm, oblong bands of light. In the middle of one of these you stop and look up. From some great distance above you, it seems higher even than the massive firs, Janice's hand descends and surrounds you, enveloping you in a gentle darkness. Then you feel yourself being lifted high above the ground, higher than you imagined possible.

PS2 Mouse Adapter

Dalia, our intern, came into work late and disheveled wearing a last-minute ponytail. I was fiddling with my computer because it had been acting up. The problem seemed to be my mouse adapter, which I suspected might have a broken or bent pin. Dalia jumped when I threw it onto the desk.

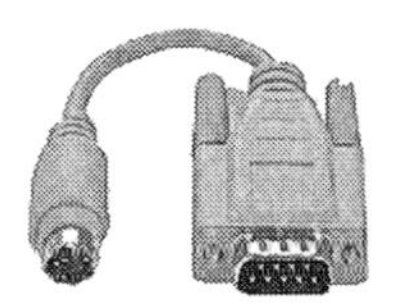

"I always have déjà vu when it comes to PS2 mouse adapters," she said. "Every single time I see one of those things I get this sense I've been here before, or I've been here for a thousand years."

She plunked her purse and musky trainers down on the floor next to my chair, leaned over me to throw her gum into my garbage pail. I smelled cigarettes on her, and nothing but affection and nostalgia coursed through me.

"I mean," she said, looking at the adapter with low-grade fear, "there's something primal, like they're bugs from the Paleozoic. Or something conjured from the collective unconscious, our lizard brains. Know what I mean?"

"Not really," I said.

"That's because you're not fully *aware*, Donald."

"I'm aware that you're a half-hour late."

Dalia and I work at a software consulting and education company whose clients are law firms. It's what's called the legal technologies industry. I write technical manuals and online tutorials for applications that facilitate the numbering and management of complex legal documents. The end users to whom I gear my writing are paralegals, legal secretaries, and attorneys. Dalia did a little bit of everything—she answered switchboard overflow, ordered office supplies, and sometimes proofread user manuals that I or my colleagues wrote. She was a recent graduate of SUNY Binghamton, and management called her an intern as an excuse to pay her seven dollars an hour. In Manhattan that might as well be sub-minimum wage. But the job market wasn't exactly booming and something is better than nothing.

She sat down on the metal folding chair on the other side of the desk we shared. Over the last few days she'd been looking over my latest creation, a reference guide for a product called U_Number, an add-on utility to Microsoft Word that eases the creation and management of numbering schemes in legal documents.

I figured it was good on all fronts to have Dalia read the technical documentation that we produced. Let her get familiar with our company style, was my thought, let her get to know the software so that she could answer a client's question in a pinch, and let her proofread, since she's good at it.

I asked her how she was coming along with the proofreading of this particular manual.

"Chapter Three, 'Security Settings,' was definitely the hottest part," she said. "But I'm afraid that the narrative voice is vegetative throughout, wouldn't you say?"

"We both know it is, but it's the nature of the material."

"'The nature of the material,'" she said, mimicking me. "You need to get a little juice in these manuals."

This was our usual banter, she the youthful provocateur, I the geeky straight man. I didn't mind, it made the day go by a little faster.

In partial recompense for her shitty salary, management agreed that she could use her work computer for her own private stuff. It was a crappy, three-year-old laptop and she brought it home at the end of every day, back in every morning. When she went out for lunch or stepped away from our desk I could smell the laptop there, putting out its Dalia and cigarette odor, like an epistle sent from her bedroom. She'd covered its case in stickers from bands I'd never heard of—the Duomo Renegades, Gladioli, The Wee Scats, Grrl Mannequins.

I tried to concentrate on the project I'd started this morning, but I could feel Dalia on the other side of the desk. She was fidgeting, shuffling something around in one of her drawers. The whole desk vibrated with her activity.

"Did I tell you that I'm working on a play?" she shot out.

"No."

"Do you want to know what it's about?"

"Not really."

"It's a about my fucked up existence and this shite job and you." Then the phone rang and she answered it, transferred the call, hit Release. "But mostly it's about you, Donald."

"Oh yeah?"

"Uh-huh. Where you go at night. Your dirty little secrets."

"You think you know my secrets? What are they?"

"You'll have to come to opening night to find out."

I have a 17 inch monitor that blocks my view of her when she sits centered and still, which is rarely. Dalia will knock on the back of the monitor if I appear to be too deeply entrenched in work as if it were a front door. "Can I borrow a cup of milk?"

Now she leaned over to one side of the monitor and said, "You look like you've aged since I last saw you."

"Since yesterday?"

I knew what she was doing, what was coming next.

"You need love, D. You need a good little cocksucker."

"Don't talk like that."

"And by the way, there's an error on page 57 of your fine creation. You wrote 'Lick the Renumber button . . . ' instead of 'Click the Renumber button . . . '"

"Good catch. Thanks."

"But you see what I'm saying?"

"No."

"That's what's on your mind. Lick lick lick. Lick lick dick."

"Please stop talking for now," I said. "We've got to prepare for the Rosen Mulch and Wood demo tomorrow morning."

"*Wood*," she said, laughing, "See?"

As the company wasn't doing particularly well these days, it was necessary to get this documentation into clients' hands if only to verify that my work and Dalia's proofreading were billable, that we were pulling our weight. I had to conduct a WebEx demo for a client so our account executives could sell classroom training on this U_Number product.

"I want you to see how I set up and run the demo," I told Dalia. "It might be a useful tool for you at some point down the road."

"Can I talk during the demo?"

"No. Just lurk."

"I'm an excellent lurker."

"Let's do a practice run in about an hour. It's important that we get everything in tip top shape beforehand. Please find those U_Number demo documents and send me the link. I want to get any wrinkles smoothed out. And I need ten minutes of silence, please."

"I've upset you."

"That's not silence," I said. "And you have not upset me."

"Neither is that."

At the time, our firm was in the process of revamping its website in the hope of drumming up, or at least maintaining, business. I represented the Content Department in after-hour meetings that took place a couple of times a week with a marketing company that was helping us with the new design.

The meetings took place well after Dalia had left with her borrowed laptop. At first her absence from the other side of our desk struck me as poignant—the lonely chair, the empty space.

But soon that emptiness moved inside of me, and I realized I missed her, that I'd fallen for her.

The site had to be both technologically sophisticated and pleasing to the eye. As with most corporate sites, ours soon contained images of successful clients interacting with our consultants—all in representation. None of the pictures were of us or our clients, of course. The images showed light-skinned African Americans, a smattering of competent looking and pretty Pan-Asians and Genero-Latinos, with a good mix of women among all groups. But at the company we were all white and almost all male, and none of us were particularly handsome. To avoid paying the marketing firm by the hour, we paid a flat fee to use a variety of their online development tools. To help determine the "mix" of people to be displayed on the site we used their proprietary DiversityBuilder tool. It consisted of a series of dialog boxes that would determine how many of the canned shots showed minorities, women and "the elderly." We'd decided to go with "Urban" as our setting, as opposed to "World" or "Heartland." We also marked the "Also include images of the Elderly" checkbox. These were not images of old men and women with walkers, wearing sweats. These were depictions of elder professionals—senior partner types, wealthy investors, seasoned entrepreneurs. Men and women who'd lived grand lives and would live on for another century or more.

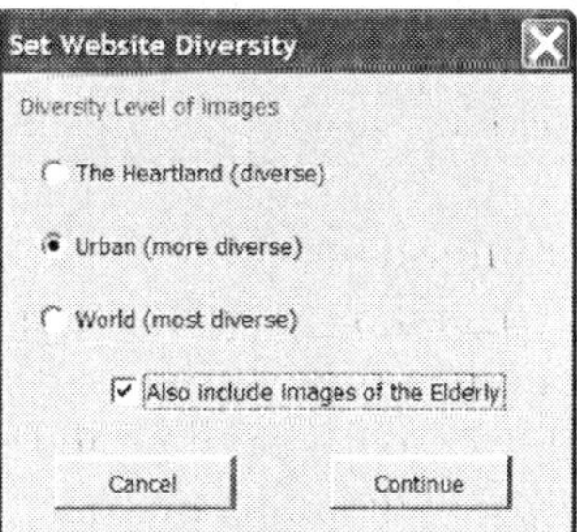

Slowly but surely the new website design began to emerge. In the end, we'd rebranded ourselves fairly crisply, with a new logo, a new font set and color scheme, a multitude of Flash modules and testimonials, and an emphasis that we were a multi-ethnic and diversity-friendly organization. Many of our clients and potential clients were among the largest law firms in the country and more than a handful were experts on litigating class action suits on behalf of the disabled, minorities, Medicaid recipients, victims of lead poisoning, silicosis, and so on. The jury was still out as to whether or not the redesigned site would increase our business, but it was a moot point. Simply put, it was necessary to have a strong Web presence if only to keep pace with our competitors in the legal technologies industry.

It was August 18, a Tuesday, when the new website was about to go live. It was hot out, and everyone showed up at the office drenched in sweat. Dalia came in, groomed, rested, smelling of lilacs.

"I have some news for you," she said.

"Yes?"

"I'm pregnant. Just barely."

I leaned to one side of my monitor and looked over at her, but all I could see was her right elbow moving up and down as she did something with her hair. She had recently adhered a small mirror to the back of my monitor.

"I mean I'm not telling my parents or any of my friends yet, but I'll bet you I'm pregnant. I'm never late, and now I'm *very* late, so there can be only one explanation."

"I don't believe you," I said.

"No, I'm totally serious." She leaned over and smiled at me. "Pregnito. Pregnistan. Pregosity."

"Jesus."

"I'll be fine."

"What are you going to do?"

"Oh, I'll keep it, if that's what you mean. I'll be a great mother."

"May I ask who the father is?"

"It's you, Donald. It's definitely you."

"Oh, *right*!"

"Seriously, I think you're the dad."

"We've never even been alone outside of this place, let alone *together*."

"I stole some of your semen."

"Where do you come up with this shit?"

"It's true. You were masturbating and I was under your bed. Afterward, you fell asleep and I used a *petite* pipette and got it right out of your navel. I put it in myself and—*voila*! I half did it to get off, though I didn't really get off. What I want to know is what you were thinking about. Was I in it?"

"I've got this stuff to do," I said.

"Okay. But for the record, I like you and your genes. I won't be upset one iota if my kid turns out to be a carbon copy of you. Though I do hope he'll get a little more action."

"Shut up," I said.

"Shutting up."

Four or five hours passed without either of us exchanging a single word. In the afternoon she said that she should've just asked me to have sex with her, instead of going to all the trouble of sneaking in. She asked, "Would you have?"

"I don't know. Working together and everything. It's complicated."

"Well it's not a relationship I want from you, anyway, with all due respect."

"Look, I know we don't pay you well enough. I get it. I try to be a good boss to you. I like you . . ."

"You *like* me?"

"Come on, Dalia. Just stop. It's not working, you've made that clear. Fine. Go home, don't come back. I'll do the paperwork. You'll qualify for unemployment. You can put me on your resume as a reference. You're unique, I'll give you that much. You're one of a kind."

"Stop with the clichés. You probably fantasize about bending me over your computer, don't you?"

A little sadness fish was now swimming around in my soul, but mostly I was pissed and a little ashamed. "Go home," I said, and I was serious.

"I can take the laptop?"

The next day Dalia came into the office as if nothing had happened.

"What are you doing here?" I said.

"I knew you were joking."

"I put in the paperwork. You shouldn't have come. It's very awkward."

Suddenly, and only for a moment, I could see her eyes getting moist, her lower lip quivering. "But this is the only job out there." Then she regained her composure and threw down her purse and took off her sneakers. She leaned over me and spit her gum into the garbage can. Her smell overcame me for a moment. I continued to look at my monitor, the sadness fish now a big grouper. She stood motionless behind me.

"Working," I said. "Go home."

She put her hand on my shoulder, leaned over, and kissed me on the cheek.

"I'm going," she said at last.

"Leave your ID behind. I forgot to ask for that yesterday." She dropped it on my keyboard then gathered up her things, tucking the laptop under her arm.

"Good luck with your play," I said, standing up, wanting to send her off with something polite and neutral.

"I'm sure it'll be great. It has been so far." She held up the pendant she'd been wearing around her neck. I'd always thought of it as some kind of steel, right-angle scrap—a kind of odd looking fob of some kind but now I could see that it was a digital voice recorder. "Eight hours fits in this little guy. So I've got all of our dialogue on it. It's been great. Every night I mine it."

"Glad to have been of service," I said. "Look, I'm sorry about this, I really am. I wish you could just control yourself a little more."

"But you'll get more done now, not having to manage me."

"I guess that's true."

I stepped forward and kissed her squarely on the lips. She didn't pull away. I put my hand on the back of her neck and pulled her into me, continuing the kiss. We were standing and could have been seen by the entire office. But I didn't care. I let go and looked around. Nobody seemed to have noticed.

"I could sue you," she said, wiping her lips softly with the back of her hand.

"And you'd win," I acknowledged.

She turned and began to walk toward the double glass doors that led to the elevator banks. Then she stopped without turning around and said, "You know where I live." And then out the doors she went.

A few days later I was taking the subway downtown to Battery Park City, heading to Dalia's. I had developed the wrong impression—how poor could the girl be if she lived down here? Then again I'd heard a thousand stories of people getting great mortgages right after 9/11 while prices were unnaturally low and fear was insufferably high.

I felt like the sucker, going into her lobby, signing in with the doorman then getting into the sparkling, brushed aluminum-paneled elevator. I hit the button for the thirtieth floor. As the elevator zoomed upward I realized that Dalia's digs would invariably be leagues above mine. In a flash the elevator halted, threw me toward the ceiling, dinged, and the doors flew open. Was I sad, ecstatic, excited, fearful? I couldn't say. I didn't know what to expect. I was released into a tortuous set of corridors and followed the plaques indicating the range that contained her apartment number. The corridors bifurcated once, then again, then again, until finally I was sweating and walking down the final hallway. I knew I was getting close because I heard *us*, our dialog, only amplified:

Oh, I'll keep it, if that's what you mean. I'll be a great mother.

May I ask who the father is?

It's you, Donald. It's definitely you.

A pause, and again:

May I ask who the father is?

It's you, Donald. It's definitely you.

We spent a few minutes looking out of her floor-to-ceiling casement windows that faced Ground Zero. The anniversary was coming up and already preparations were underway for the return of the Twin Towers of Light in an adjacent parking lot. We could see a small crew down there milling around some generator trucks and rack upon rack of giant spotlights.

"I'm sorry about all the theater at work," she said. "I used to be medicated. And before that I was not medicated but supervised, as in one step away from institutionalized."

"You don't usually seem so bad to me, just excitable," I said. "And unwilling to play by the rules. You end up getting people awfully confused."

"I'm not really so bad anymore, actually. I just don't belong anywhere, don't fit in. The world always seemed tilted to me, reality has always been a porous concept. I could see things that I couldn't believe others were blind to."

"Can I have something to drink?"

She went and poured me a glass of bourbon and distilled water, filled her own glass with distilled water.

"The purest thing going," she said, holding up the plastic container on which the silhouette of an iron was printed.

I nodded. "This is a beautiful apartment. Your parents bought it for you?"

"It's my brother's," she said and then didn't seem to want to talk about it. "God, I want a cigarette but I'm trying to quit because of the little one."

"Oh?"

"That at least was the truth." She lifted up her t-shirt, took my hand, and placed it over her belly button ring.

"You're flat as a washboard," I said. Her skin was warm, dry.

"I know. I keep waiting for a little bit of swelling or something."

"You were saying, about seeing things that others are blind to."

"Well, for one thing, I know when deception is going on in any form. It seems to me that people are lying to everyone in sight, including themselves, and they're doing this at all times. Even you do it, which is especially distressing."

"But I'm just kind of normal." Then, out of nowhere, I felt myself getting a little riled up, emotions filling me up in a way I hadn't expected. "I mean I'm nothing. Nothing special at all. I've got my music, my handful of friends, my wine, my job, sometimes women, but there's not much else in my life."

"But you were there."

"There?"

"You were there at work all day, just sitting in front of me. I respect that constancy."

"And you were there sitting in front of me."

"It was circumstantial, see? I know it sounds a little intimidating, but it's going to turn out fine."

"What *it* are you referring to?"

"The baby," she said, rubbing her belly.

"That you got from my stolen semen?"

"I know how things are going to stack up with this. Based on the way things are now, I know they're going to be okay down the road. Causality in reverse. The truth is, I didn't really want to say all that much to you about my plan, but I couldn't shut my fat trap that morning. You're so self-satisfied sometimes. I had to tell you I was there in your little dank cocoon of an apartment."

"I don't believe you were there, you know that, right?"

We went to her sofa and sat on opposite ends, as if we were expecting someone to fill the space between us.

"I once saw you on the subway when you didn't know I was there," she said. "It was late, the 4 or 5 going out to Brooklyn. You looked distressed hanging onto a pole. There were plenty of seats but for some reason you insisted on standing. And then I realized that you punish yourself all the time. Not in big ways, but you must be carrying around something big, because you never let yourself take the easy route."

"I stand on the train because I sit all day."

"You were exhausted, honey. I don't know what was going on, but you had these circles under your eyes. Of all the times I wanted to just take you by the hand, that was the most tempting. But it was even *more* tempting to observe you."

"How kind."

"You must have been thinking of a girl, based on your expression."

"Probably was. Women are a lot of work."

"You make it that way. You're a born tech writer, through and through. Always trying to sort things out, plumb the depths, organize, find the most efficient procedure instead of letting things be."

"In that case, why in the world would you want me to be the father of your hypothetical kid?"

"Because one shouldn't let go of things, one *should* analyze his surroundings, one *should* be distressed at all times given how messy the world has become. *You* never tune out. Never ever."

I went to the little island between her kitchen and living room and filled my glass with bourbon. I brought back the plastic container of distilled water and refilled her glass. When I leaned over her I noticed she was wearing her little necklace, the digital voice recorder.

"You recording all of this?" I said.

"Of course. The script is going to knock everyone's socks off."

"But is all of this," I pointed to my heart, then to hers, "Is all of this real? I mean are we talking about stuff that's really happening or have you staged this?"

"Oh, you poor thing," and she took my hand. "You now see exactly what I'm saying about you, don't you? Just let go. What's the difference?"

"For one, either you're having a kid or you're not."

"Either I'm having a kid on stage or I'm having a kid in reality."

"Mostly, I operate in reality."

"Let it go," she said, pulling me back onto the sofa so that we were pressed into each other. "Let it go."

Port Authority (Part I)

I was waiting for the subway around midnight when I noticed this kid standing right next to me on the platform. He was in his late teens or early twenties, probably Hispanic, with acne scars and pencil-thin sideburns. He fidgeted, turned to look at me when I wasn't looking at him, and then looked away when I caught him doing it. Finally he turned to me and said, "What stop for the Port Authority bus terminal?"

"Thirty-Fourth Street," I said. It came out reflexively. This was at the Eighth Street stop in Manhattan and I was on my way to my job as a legal proofreader to work the graveyard shift. The problem was, at this moment I still hadn't recovered from an evening out I just had with a couple of friends, and my head was swimming.

"They don't just have Greyhound there, right?" he said. "They got all the other buses?"

"All the buses, that's right," I said.

I stepped back from the tracks when the R train pulled in, and we got on together. At the Twenty-Eighth Street stop I told the Hispanic kid that the next stop was his. "You'll have to walk a few blocks west underground, so you don't even have to go outside." He didn't say anything to me, but he still seemed a little nervous when he got off.

About a second after the train doors closed, I realized I'd probably told him to get off at the wrong stop. Wasn't it clear as day that the Port Authority bus terminal was at Forty-Second Street, not Thirty-Fourth? In fact, yes, in fact I'd given him the wrong directions. When I got off at Fifty-Seventh Street I checked a map on the station wall and there was Port Authority, where it has always been, on West Forty-Second Street.

I walked four blocks to the office building where I work, took the elevator, booted up the computer, logged in, and, downing one cup of coffee after another, proofread legal contracts until the sun rose over Seventh Avenue.

A few nights later I was walking to my spot on the subway platform when I noticed that same kid standing there. I didn't want to deal with it and turned away, but he let loose one of those stadium whistles that stopped me in my tracks.

"I was going up to Detroit," he said. "My great-grandmother died. She was a hundred. One hundred years old. Because of you I missed the service and almost missed the burial."

He was twenty feet away and shouting.

"Do I know you?" I said, feigning befuddlement.

He started walking toward me. I decided I should walk toward him as well so as not to seem cowed and to initiate some kind of mirror symmetry, which can be amusing with the right partner. The few midnight commuters between us stepped out of our path.

"Ah yes, now I remember. I sent you to the wrong stop. Well, I was drunk," I said, smiling, as if this were the ultimate, inviolate excuse. "I should've sent you to Forty-Second, no?"

"Yes," he said, "and it didn't take me long to find out. I missed the bus and then I missed most of the funeral."

"Yes, I got it," I said. "That's too bad."

"It doesn't matter. Not to my great-grandmother. She's dead, right?"

The hope of a brawl seemed to be getting some of our fellow travelers excited and they were watching to see what happened next. Among them was a good-looking woman doctor, or doctor impersonator, wearing two stethoscopes around her pearly neck. Her blond hair was done up in a loose bun like an eighties porn star. Beyond her, a big guy done up in muddy construction worker garb looked shaken to the core, literally, as if he'd been using a jackhammer for the last twenty-four hours. He was shooting what I'd call an invitation in my direction. His eyes were devoid of much in the way of affection, but I got his meaning. I had a feeling that if a fight broke out, he'd back me.

Then the misdirected kid got closer and looked at my face, like he could see something crawling on it. Okay, I thought, don't flinch—let him throw the first punch.

"Do you have dry skin?" he said.

"What?" I said.

"Your skin is flaking off your face. You need some moisturizer."

"I don't know," I said.

"I can get you some high grade moisturizer from a top U.S. firm," he said.

"Like I said, I'm sorry about the directions, but let's leave it at that."

"How much do you pay for toothpaste?" the kid said.

Christ, I thought, he's sort of a genius for turning this around so quickly. Here I was worried that I'd have to fight for the first time in twenty-five years, and here he was commercially capitalizing on that fear. A real American. I knew where this was heading.

"I'm not interested in Amway," I said.

"This is *not* Amway. I'm talking about a local business venture. A minority venture."

"No thanks," I said. With that I walked away and got on the first car when the train came.

The last thing I heard him say was, "Pets?"

I didn't see him for another week or so, but then there he was again at the platform, at the same spot, wearing tri-colored alligator skin shoes, designer jeans, and a hound's-tooth sports jacket, under which a tight-fitting mock turtleneck showed he had some pecs. His skin looked good. The few purple scars, remnants, I guessed, of adolescent acne, seemed to have faded to almost nothing at all. His hair, black and lustrous, was thick and started low on his forehead, came down to a little widower's peak.

At his side was a petite Japanese woman who, in turn, had a sort of extra-dimensional, brightly-hued cart-on-wheels by her side. He saw me from a distance, said something to her, and she locked the wheels on the cart with her foot. She opened some of the drawers and inspected their contents with faked interest as I headed past them to my usual spot. The subway pulled in almost immediately and I, hoping to escape, was about to step on when the kid placed a hand on each of my shoulders and eased me back.

"I've got something to show you," he said.

The train door closed an inch from my face.

"Your skin may not be so bad after all," he shouted over the diminishing din of the train, "but what Michiko and I are sensing is that your attitude is all wrong. We don't have anything for that, per se. Nothing *topical*, that is. But we do have—"

"I'm not interested," I interrupted.

"What we do have are intelligent nanotubes."

He motioned to Michiko, who adroitly drew forth from one of the more brightly luminescing drawers of her cart a cylinder with a cork in one end. She removed the cork with her teeth and handed the cylinder to her partner.

"We're administering them on a test basis, gratis," he said.

"I have to get to work," I said, "And now I've got to wait for another goddamned train."

"These," he said, holding up the vial, "are straight from Murray Hill, New Joisey. Fell off the back of an electron microscope. Know what's in Murray Hill, New Joisey?"

I turned and began walking to the other end of the platform, which seemed to be continually extending out into the subway tunnel at the same pace at which I progressed.

"Bell Laboratories," I heard the kid shout in answer to his own question.

Michiko was soon walking behind me in her flats. She asked me to please stop for just one moment so she could say something. Her voice, half stumbling English and half cartoon girlishness, persisted. The exit sign was a few yards ahead. I should have just kept going.

"Just turn please to show that you are a gentle man," she said.

I turned.

She held forth an atomizer and misted me with a few pumps of her pointer finger.

★ ★ ★

I was on my back on a station bench and a young woman leaned over me, her t-shirt brushing against my face. She smelled like cigarettes, alcohol, and something earthy. Her pants were speckled with what looked like beet and carrot juice stains. I looked at her groin and her thick military belt that missed every other loop, at her low-riders that she wore too low even for their name, at her little roll of a belly and flattened navel, at the head of a snake tattoo peeking up from her pubis.

"Oh, you're *up*," she said.

She was looking in the direction of my feet with her hand deep in my inside jacket pocket.

"Take it easy, mister. You're ill. I was looking for your I.D."

My mouth was filled with bile and grit. My bowels felt like maybe they'd been violated. I held her arm.

"You're beginning to hurt me." She spoke with a British accent.

"Nanotubes," I said. "They put them in me. In my mouth or nose. Or in my asshole."

"Please let go of me," she said.

I let go.

She unhooked her cell phone from a thin wire that ran down the front of her pants. She was still for a moment, looking at me with either suspicion or pity. Her irises were variegated blue and green. The blue was grayish; the green was bluish.

"I can call 911. You need to go to hospital."

"'*The*,'" I said, "and nonsense. Help me up."

She had short dark hair with a magenta streak, and she wore ironic, garish eyeliner. That navel of hers was opening and closing as she moved around, frowning and smiling, making O's as if astonished with the world. Oh shit, did I ever feel like crap. I looked down. My belt was hitched, but on a looser setting than usual. I now felt certain that things were crawling around inside of me, from the mouth down, from my rectum up.

What would happen when they met?

The girl's name was Desi or Daisy. She wouldn't set foot inside the foyer of my building. I don't really blame her. Brits, how well behaved they are. Lovely of her to walk me home; brilliant of her to keep a nice hold on my elbow the whole way. She struck me as organic, fully edible.

I figured the Hispanic kid with the alligator shoes had it in for me once he saw me the second time. Didn't like being so blithely misdirected by a Vandyked kike with John Lennon glasses. So he decided to punish me, and maybe I deserved it. Only I didn't feel so bad anymore.

When I got back up to my apartment I called in sick to Joel, who runs my shift at the law firm. He's an opera singer by day and gets a decent number of off-Broadway gigs that don't pay the bills. Then I went to the bathroom and took a very large crap, a cathartic crap. The toilet jammed and I had to take the plunger to it. I had to laugh. My goddamn bowels are such good harbingers of my emotional state of affairs that I can tell when a fit of depression is coming on because I shit like a little primate—a marmoset or something—when things are at their darkest. But tonight I was obviously feeling magnanimous, open to possibilities, a real go-getter. Well, I thought, intelligent nanotubes or not, let me see what the night shall bring forth.

How can I explain the spell that came over me, that drove my actions? Minute by minute, I was in control—true. Yet, behind it all, an end-game had been imprinted upon some gauzily obscured level of my consciousness, an end-game to which I could not gain access. It was as if some glue-sniffing bloke had hotwired my soul and was behind the controls of my mind.

I ironed an Egyptian cotton shirt, showered, and decided I should feed the cats, who seemed agitated and were nipping at my ankles for attention. "What?" I asked the cats after they ignored the freshly presented wet food. "*What*?" But the cats following me around had apparently not indicated what it normally had—that they were hungry. The two of them looked at me with wide eyes and filled the air with high-pitched mews for some other reason. But what was it? That feline perceptions clearly trump human ones was a worry; that sporadically throughout the ages these little furry beasts had been thought to be in league with the devil or other pagan and dark forces only added to my concern. I love them, naturally, but could they sense in me something deathly or evil, half-monster, bitter-smelling, despairing?

I looked at myself in the person-sized mirror. I looked okay. Nothing special. Standard skinny but solid built guy, average height, curly hair sprouting from his shoulders, beard beginning to get gray in it. Maybe ten percent gray. My pupils, on close inspection, were fully dilated, which was unusual.

On the other side of the apartment I could hear one of the cats digging litter in its shitbox.

I felt clean inside and out, sharp, no clouds of doubt obscuring my thoughts. Look into your own eyes, I commanded myself, and leaned forward. A planet in each one. But deeper, inside my mind, there were not many thoughts at all. I wanted. I wanted. I wanted *something*. Nothing but an odd emptiness resided within me, I had to admit. A desirous sort of *something*. In particle physics it might have been the manifestation of an undiscovered particle whose near speed-of-light collision gives rise to paradoxes thus far unimagined. Anti-space folded within lust, wrapped in layers of longing.

Then something more disturbing happened, a brief dash of an event that I'm embarrassed to pass along. I'd recently switched the cats over to a fancy sort of food because I'd gotten a two thousand dollar per year raise and thought, why not share the wealth? So for the last week I'd been feeding them things like Organic Lamb Stew and Hearty Halibut and the like. The problem was that in my disturbed state the fresh turds my cat had just released into the litter smelled good. I mean they smelled edible in a pungent way, like corned beef hash frying in a cast iron skillet. I immediately recognized that something was awry, that a short circuit had occurred, some tripped up crossover from my olfactory center into my food-imaging center. I cut off the urge to actually take a fork and stick it in the shit, but it was too late to stop the desire to eat something as odoriferous as high-class cat turds. I looked in the fridge and cupboards, and the only thing that struck my fancy was a little can of expensive capanada, which I opened and began eating with the two-finger scoop.

I opened my window and stuck my head outside. It had been drizzling for days and the streets, though essentially quiet so late at night, gave echo to footsteps and the occasional taxi spinning out on the wet asphalt. I was going out there, into the night, revved up, feeling some large and growing-larger emptiness inside of me that needed filling. An emptiness with mass, a paradoxical space, a ravenous desire that was both armless and legless. I was being driven by the bloke, and where he'd take me I wasn't sure.

Smile. Head on out.

The Gallery

My fate was determined by a visit, years ago, to the spiral Gallery, a structure no longer standing. Some weeks before that visit, a sculpture of prurient content had reportedly become part of the Gallery's collection. An apocryphal tale had circulated about a band of ragged art historians who had bought the sculpture, of unknown age and provenance, attributable to some great *anonymous*, and installed it in the middle of the night. All but the least respectable papers ignored the story. But according to those few twenty-five cent dailies that picked it up, the "X-rated" sculpture was simply part of an effort by the Gallery's steering committee to stave off bankruptcy by whatever means possible. It was seen as an ill-conceived act of desperation by an institution that was for the most part dead. There was suspicion that promoters had hoped that by veiling the piece's installation in mystery they would in fact draw crowds. Whatever the intent, crowds never did materialize, and the Gallery's fate seemed sealed.

The popularity of the Gallery's architectural spiral and the myth that it effected hallucinations on its visitors had long since worn off. The strange and secretive design was now said to simply amplify thoughts and moods, rather than cause visions. According to the *New York Times*, that spiral hallway "texturized meaning," but did nothing more. Some theorized that because its great hall was shaped like the cochlea, the Gallery's amplification of sound was no surprise. Holdovers from previous decades spoke more generally, often with mist in their eyes, of holy convergences and the like, space that broke the rules of a Cartesian universe. But no matter what one believed, it was an undeniably decrepit building, fading quickly, and a poorly managed, insolvent institution. Many of the greatest works of art had been pulled and were now displayed farther uptown at those monolithic institutions whose endowments seem never to be in doubt.

For decades the Gallery was an eyesore on lower Madison Avenue. It was built in the early 1920s by a trio of brothers, the mysterious Nahmans. Mysterious because they left no records of their lives, nor is it known where they went once their great building was completed. They were obsessed, so the Gallery's official history went, with creating a space unlike any other on the planet, and by most measures they succeeded. It's known only that the Nahmans' roots ran deep into Spain, to the medieval Catalonian city of Gerona. That city, its ancient section walled, its streets furrowed with narrow passages, is widely regarded as a birthplace of Kabala.

On that day of my first visit I was merely looking for some excitement. A bachelor of limited means, I sought out stimulation when things got dull, which was often. I had been working for some time in the state filing department of a large property casualty insurance company. If I recall correctly, my job involved analysis and facilitation with respect to the Company's compliance with statutes and regulations that govern insurance rates, rules, and forms. As an example (again, trusting my distant recollection), if I was told that the Company wished to begin writing general liability coverage for chicken feed manufacturers in Minnesota, I would consult the *State Filing Handbook* ("The Bible"), see what one had to do in order to request adoption of rates, rules and forms in that state for said line of business, then follow the procedures exactingly. I would correspond with the Minnesota Insurance Department for perhaps three months, and if things went swimmingly, we would soon be insuring myriad chicken feed manufacturers in that state. Simply put, it was a job—not thrilling or glorious in the least, yet above what I had expected out of life.

I picked a midweek afternoon to visit the Gallery. I guessed that attendance would be lower than on weekends and that my search for this mysterious sculpture would therefore be less inhibited. My plan was to take a long lunch. As I got off the bus at East Twenty-Third Street and looked north up Madison Avenue at my destination, I was reminded, quite clearly, that the Gallery, its resolute dome stained with rust, its concrete patches of the previous decades discolored, was nothing more than a decrepit landmark, ironically "loved" by New Yorkers in the know and ignored by all but the most post-modern of tourists. Scaffolding had been erected over the sidewalk to protect pedestrians from debris that occasionally sloughed off the façade.

I entered through the heavy brass doors, paid the fifteen dollars admission, and handed my circular ticket to the usher, who had the unfortunate duty of dressing like a medieval steward of some unknown variety. He smiled warily at me and into the great, singular hall I stepped. Those who have visited the Gallery will recall that its main architectural feature is the one continuous turn that leads always to the right at a slight declination. On the left wall—the outside wall—sculptures were displayed, some on low pedestals, others, massive, glowered from great heights. On that day, the first of numerous visits, such works were an inconsequential blur, for I was interested in only the one piece of work I'd read about. It's sad, really, to admit that I felt a stirring, an expectant and bodily palpitation. Paintings, which hung along the right, or inside wall, were of almost no interest to me: some lesser landscapes of the Hudson River schools; a few small reproductions of sketches by Goya; an abstract portrait of our famed mayor Fiorello La Guardia—these are some of the works I had my back to that day. I gave each sculpture a quick glance, not being sure whether the rumored piece was a literal rendering or a figurative sort of interpretation. As I walked farther into that space, that continuous curve, at first intriguing me with its subtle clockwise charm, was now becoming sharper, turning with an ever increasing period. On I walked, deeper into, and onward toward the center of that strange and breathtaking space.

Finally, I came upon the piece. Unlike the other works, there was no etched plastic plaque, no indication of its origin or date of composition. Mounted on a thin stand that was nearly invisible, it seemed to hover in the air in front of my face. It was strange, to say the least, to see this piece of natural ingenuity removed from the haven of thighs, perineum, navel. This shimmering sculpture made of a solid yet mysterious material, wrought with delicate precision, glimmered luridly under the display lights. Fawning, engorged, two-feet in width—all in all, daunting. A gynecological still life, both titillating and repulsive. I breathed heavily with the exertion and strangeness of my search, and I was immersed in a sea of murmuring whose source I could not locate.

Things soon began to change. I felt as if a low-frequency vibration were passing through my body, as if I were part of a conduit. I could feel sweat gathering around my upper lip and along the lines of my forehead—the sweat of nervousness and dementia. Not since I had been an adolescent, during a mid-night fit in which, bolt upright in bed, I realized that death was inevitable and my life's memories would be extinguished forever and ever once I died, had I felt this kind of sweating. I had the feeling that heavy foreplay was about to begin, felt the expectant flush of fornication. My lunch hour had already officially come and gone and I was worried, slightly, about spending much more time here. Still, I wanted badly to reach out and caress the sculpture.

I turned and looked back down the hall to see if any spectators were about. Nobody to be found close by, the great hall unwinding, curving out of sight to the left. Empty. I went back and pressed my hand against the cold rim. I set off some type of modest proximity alarm. It beeped politely, and a red light the size of a button blinked solemnly from high above. I moved closer, rubbing the engorged lips, trying to warm them. They seemed to embrace me back, to warm to the touch, although I am still uncertain if their pliancy was an illusion. A few people, defeated and perturbed by their long spiraling trek, did eventually come around that tight bend, but upon seeing me they retreated, walking backward, their eyes wide. I had that part of the great hall to myself.

From the topmost reaches of the sculpture a smooth little knob was peeking out from beneath its hood—a cautious turtle, a Cambrian arthropod. I anointed it with the last bit of moisture on my fingertips. I closed my eyes and pressed on it, rubbed that region and imagined a forty-foot tall woman bucking with pleasure. And just then a sound occupying all octaves rose from some small distance farther along the Gallery hall, welling up from an abyss. It was a mechanical activation of sorts but without comparison to anything I'd ever heard. A deep rumble of bearings followed by the sound of air rushing through a narrow fissure at great pressure.

Things seemed different now in the gallery. The alarm had stopped and all murmuring had ceased. Stranger still, security still hadn't showed up. A bright light, emanating from around the tight curve and reflecting off the white wall, now illuminated the sculpture. I walked toward the light source and realized with amazement that the sculpture I'd been so intimate with was the last piece of art in the Gallery. That spiral hallway was near its end, turning in upon itself in tighter and tighter proportions until a man could no longer walk it. At that narrow end I squeezed my body in as far as it could go and saw, at the edge of my vision, a bright vertical slit. The very end of the Gallery. This narrow opening—a passageway for a circus thin man—was the source of the light. I reached my hand toward it, pushing my shoulders into the fold, emptying my lungs of air. With my arm and fingers outstretched as much as possible I could feel warmth at the tip of my fingers and a gentle breath tickling the hair on my arms. But the entranceway was slowly closing, the walls gently ejecting me back into the greater width of the hallway. I quickly returned to the sculpture and slowly caressed that button until I heard the opening of the passageway once again.

I did not hesitate this time.

★ ★ ★

I neither fell nor rose, floated nor sank, sped through tunnels nor was entombed in ectoplasm. I simply vanished, was reduced to a moment, a molecule, a paradox. Consciousness left me. It was, I presume, like major surgery. One moment I was there, the next, the thing had been done.

I was now a newborn being delivered into a smoke-filled New Orleans room on September 16, 1965, my birthday. I was still coated in the stuff of uterine arrival when my umbilical cord was adeptly snipped and tied off by a hand still unknown to me.

"Oh Christ, Dora," I heard a woman's voice say (this would be my Aunt Julie), "he's a little troublemaker, I can see it in those eyes. And a horny one, ain't he?"

"Like his father," said another voice (this was indeed my father, who never stuck around after this day).

A small crowd was gathered in the room. I was now fully conscious, my mind that of the thirty-seven year old who had entered the Gallery moments earlier, yet I was unable to communicate with anything but the most infantile and shattering of squeals, one of which I let out. This scene was to be repeated myriad times, and the invariability of each rebirth brought the utmost comfort to me.

I will never know the exact parameters of the Gallery's mystical machinations nor question the facilitating role of the prurient sculpture. Was God looking for a good trick to play, or had the Nahman's, those immortal triplets, laid the groundwork with Kabalistic lamentations lost to the ages? None of that matters. The Gallery had become my redeemer, the recycler of mortality. I knew that as long as I could make it to age thirty-seven or thereabouts, that as long as I could access the mysterious piece of artwork on its pedestal, I could activate the portal. How many times have I gone through this process? I cannot be certain, since my memory capacity is only that of a mortal who might, if lucky, see a century of life.

My peculiar life has been spent accruing knowledge, memorizing the most spectacular stock performers and the events leading to the most disastrous failings of humanity. Passing through after refining my knowledge of a particular regional crisis, I would hope to change the path of our world for the better. But inevitably I would fail in all but the most mundane of tasks, that of making money. For the world, its course firmly set in motion, can be affected only fractionally by a single person of unremarkable lineage, despite his wisdom above years. And a repetitious life, especially with near perfect foresight, is invariably a somewhat dull endeavor.

Fresh from the uterus, I was hungry, cold, and irritable. As my mother, the Dora of above, tenderly fed me the first drops of breast milk, my tiny mind would race ahead, planning my leverage of foreknowledge, tallying my potential wealth, plotting my foreshortened life's stratagem for this go around. And then, also invariably, baby's meconium came forth and there the small gathering of young hippies gave a unified cheer and my mother held me high into a cloud of tobacco smoke, saying, weakly, "My little king! You're going to be my little fucking king." Indeed, I would be.

Always, that spring day of renewal commenced with my dreamy march down the worn gallery hallway toward that secreted button around which, I am now certain, the universe spun. The first year or more of my renewed life was invariable. I was happy to be swaddled, changed, fed, bathed, coddled, consciously savoring these times. In order to keep suspicion at bay, I could not feasibly do anything to affect my life or the world until I had reached at least two years of age. Needless to say, it would be physically impossible, nearly, to do otherwise.

It was odd, for example, to spy within the financial pages of the newspaper the chart of a stock whose every peak and trough I knew by heart. This is not information I could, at that age, state clearly, nor even fully comprehend in the sense an adult might. Yet I knew what I was seeing and knew the look of that chart as I knew the smell of my own sour diapers. I would be consuming mushy peas that my mother was gently forcing down my gullet, when, at the sight of the chart on the floor (the newspaper pages had been laid out to protect the Linoleum from my feeding), I would twist my head, go wide eyed and begin drooling, then hoop and haw with excretory force. My mother, a woman who would never have to work another day in her life by the time I was ten, would say, "Baby like figgers? Look at all the figgers lined up in columns!" She would lift that page from the floor and hold it to my face, an action for which she ceaselessly credits herself as setting me on my course toward financial indomitability.

After a handful of passes through the Gallery's portal I was maximizing my knowledge of stocks, bonds, wars, women, minerals, and oil. Women, though thrown into the midst of the list, should perhaps be entirely excluded, for no matter how many times I had lived my years, I had not been able to improve upon a certain highly competent mediocrity when it comes to the act itself. I was, and am, still the same physical specimen, able only to perfect the mechanics of lovemaking, but unable to change who I *am*; although I gain knowledge, I am still Jonathan S., moderately handsome, shy sometimes to a fault, and rarely the sort of lover women swoon over. Nonetheless, during those uncountable repetitious years, I am proud to say, I was a selfless and competent provider of pleasure to numerous women, or instances of women (for many were repeats).

It was not long in terms of my course of lives before I began encountering, on a recurring basis, a female who, I surmised, must also have discovered the secret of episodic repetitions, for I saw her grow closer to me with each new life I lived. Perhaps we were mutually circling each other, neither certain of the other's provenance, both hesitant to ascertain the truth girding the fellow traveler. While I always knew at what point I would encounter all my other acquaintances for the first time, she shifted about in the otherwise predictable timeline. At first she was a matter of curiosity, appearing momentarily in my life and then disappearing, once, at my insistence, even joining me for a cup of coffee in my later years as if we were acquaintances by some other means. This was early on, and neither of us was willing to ask the one important question that was so absurd as to be a reasonable cause for institutionalization, a chance not worth taking given the unknown lifespan of the decrepit Galley that housed the all important portal. To be removed from the possibility of cycling through one's life again was unthinkable and I suppose akin to death. In one life we might greet each other with toothy smiles at a polo game and retire to a willow's shade to sip Meursault. I recall a visit to one of my bankers in which she and I greeted each other in an antechamber as if we were the closest of friends, even though we had never met in that life.

As time, or *our* time, went on we would make our presence known to each other at earlier and earlier stages of development. Of age roughly equal to mine, I had met her this last time at the city's top private grammar school where we had both managed to win full scholarships. We became companions, the best of friends until, in our teen years, the dam finally burst and we decided to marry as soon as was legally permissible.

It turned out that she, Alice, had been a cleaning woman at the Gallery. One night, piqued by the verisimilitude of the new sculpture, stimulated by its quiet proximity, and, as always, diligent in her work habits, she thoughtfully varnished the intimate region with a moistened cloth.

We waited for some time before having our first child. We now have three, the eldest being seven and the youngest not yet one. They are mortal, delicate things, and in need of Ivy League educations. We could not bear to leave them nor to leave each other for another pass through that spiral Gallery, even with knowledge of certain reunion, and so we allowed time to pass until, inevitably, the old Gallery was emptied, demolished, and a glass tower, a residential high rise, erected in its place. Only yesterday we stood before the finished behemoth, acknowledging together the certainty of our mortality.

We will live out the rest of our years without hope of renewal, our vast knowledge being carried only forward until it is taken into the grave with us. Our physicians inform us that we appear to be psychologically oversensitive with regard to the effects of aging. With fear and awe I have counted several dozen gray hairs in my beard. Aging is an alien and frightening experience. Although we have lived for millennia, we have no experience with the inexorability of physical decline. And if we are encyclopedic beyond our apparent years, we are like frightened children when it comes to reading the newspapers each morning. We never know what new darkness the headlines will report. When you've known everything that is to come, knowing nothing of what is to come is a terrifying prospect. To alleviate this tension, Alice has decided to take up tennis. Given my years, I'm surprised I never even considered the game.

At the Laundromat

Before the women flee they pin down or secure their sleeves, collars, overcoats, scarves and any loose fabric that can be grabbed, since I'd be the one doing the grabbing. "Don't go, oh god, don't leave me!" I've said so many times that I should have cards printed up that say it. I've seen their backs as they hopped into taxis or run down cross streets with stockinged feet, shoes in hand, as they've escaped like stumbling drunks down blind alleyways in the rain, as they've run into strange bars or the lobbies of buildings within which they know not a soul, all just to prevent me from grabbing at their sleeves or skirt, their cuffs or hems, their belt loops, all so that they won't have to hear me ask for love, a little more time, one more *real* conversation.

As soon as I see those pins shimmering in the moonlight I know the relationship's over and all I can do is try to prove them wrong this one last time by remaining silent, aloof, as still as a statue as they walk away. But soon my heart starts banging around in my chest cavity and my girl leaves with not a single bit of loose fabric with which to be drawn back into my embrace. Even her hair is up and in a tight bun, or under a hat that's pinned down. Tight and smooth as a mannequin, she walks away. There goes her back. How very many backs I've seen.

The solution? "Go to a shrink," as my last girlfriend, tall Arlene, said, "and tell him you want to learn how to *let go* of women and before you know it the women won't let *you* go."

She was wearing a Blue Collar brand t-shirt when she said this, its short sleeves duct-taped to her slender upper arms. She inhaled, exhaled, then leaned over to give me one final peck on the neck—a sweet gesture—which is when I saw, perched before my very eyes, her shiny, complex little ear. I took it between my fingers, like a piece of under-ripe fruit. I could feel a faint click as the ridge of cartilage beneath the skin deformed. "Please please . . . ." I began, as usual. She jumped back then raised a hand to her ear, pressing it against her skull.

"I hadn't thought about the ears," she said, and walked away.

I found my therapist, Dr. H. Lowencross, in a tear-off ad on the bulletin board of my laundromat, over which he had his practice. The ads made a good point—why not get your laundry started then go upstairs for a session?

As it turned out, Dr. Lowencross was built something like me, which is to say fairly large, though no giant. There the similarities ended. He was slightly duck-footed and had the sort of lively sympathetic eyes and open face that made you want to pour your guts out onto the floor right in front of him. More than just sympathetic, his eyes were wide-set, so that when he looked past me in thought he gave the impression of seeing something at a tremendous distance. The window behind him framed several tenements and, peeking up from above them, a church steeple. By adjusting the angle at which I looked at him, and squinting a little, I could make it look as if he were wearing the steeple for a hat. He was so still when he spoke that this illusion could sometimes last several minutes.

In our first meeting I described my dilemma regarding neediness and grasping for clothing, and was leading up to the point at which tall Arlene had recommended I seek help.

"Tell me something about how you do your laundry," he interrupted. "Tonight, for example. You have started your load downstairs?"

"Yes."

"Do you separate whites and colors?"

I nodded.

"Bleach?"

"On my undershirts—if they're developing stains in the armpits."

"And your other whites, such as athletic socks and underwear?"

"No. Bleach destroys elastic."

"Aha."

"Yes Doctor?"

"You value a snug fit more than you do whiteness, which represents purity. What does this mean to you in a larger sense?"

"I like my clothing to last. I don't like underwear sliding off my hips or socks crumpling up below my ankles."

"Yes, if you are speaking metaphorically I could not agree more."

"I'm speaking literally, Doc."

"And in doing so you are revealing a trait that may undermine your relationships: you are a literal man. When a woman comes to you implying that she wants to be with you, you infer from her behavior that she wishes to be with you *and only you*—forever. Is that right?"

"What happens is: I don't want to let her go. I fall in love with her too easily and want to be able to stick my nose in her hair and smell its honeyed loveliness at any hour of the night, on any night of the week. If she's beautiful and smells good it's all I can think about."

"Many people would be envious of your enthusiasm, your," and he looked into the grave distance wearing his church steeple hat, "certitude."

"But none of my relationships have lasted for more than six months."

"Just as you require that your underwear and socks fit you snugly, so you feel a woman should also be close to you, snugly, at all times. When you feel this fit is in doubt you begin to experience a form of separation anxiety and pull her closer to you. In turn, this frightens her and she initiates the exact process that most terrifies you, that of separation. You correctly interpret her intent instantaneously (you expect it no less) and your fearful, needy grip only increases. You pull her closer still and naturally she now recoils in an unambiguous manner. Before long you have reached a fevered pitch from which recovery is not possible. Thus a self-perpetuating cycle is enacted time and again."

"You might be on to something here."

"Yes," he said, encouraged, "you cannot bare to see your socks slide down your ankles. It's very irritating, isn't it?"

"I'd use the word 'distracting.'"

"And so a woman who moves away from you, who slides off of you in an uncertain or loose-fitting fashion—if there is even a hint of uncertainty—makes you uncomfortable and distracts you. It is not enough for you. You need the *closeness*. And so as she loosens her elastic grip on you, your anxiety blossoms like wildflowers on a fertile valley slope."

"Whoa," I said.

A woman, I wanted to say, is not the same as a piece of clothing. But as far as analogies go, maybe Lowencross was spot on. Why did I insist on such closeness? Why cloy these women into a corner until they lashed out at me?

I went home that night thinking about Arlene, how she always misted herself with sage oil extract before we had sex, the way her breath smelled like the bottom of a cork (she did like her wine), how she had probably never owned any duct tape until she met me. I missed her more than I missed most of my ex-'s, and I wondered what special curse allowed me to successfully pursue such a beautiful woman and then so predictably drive her off.

I live with a cat named Polka Dot. I've always thought of her as a reflection of myself—of what I might be if I were feline. As one girlfriend surmised, perhaps this is no mere coincidence, maybe we're bound to be reincarnated as our own pets—thus one caresses one's future self. In any case, that night after my first session with Lowencross I microwaved some leftover rice and beans and threw an overripe avocado into the mix. I could see Polka Dot from across the apartment perched on the windowsill staring at me, waiting for me to call her, and when I did, she came trotting over as if no greater moment existed in her lifetime. She jumped up on my lap, purring, and looked up at me between my jostling elbows as I ate, her pupils as wide as the cosmos. You could almost see galaxies inside of them. But so what? I suddenly thought. When you look into those pupils you're not looking for galaxies, you're just thinking, look what a clueless animal I have before me, look what passes for love in her world. It's no way to live, feline or human.

"Fifty thousand years ago," Lowencross said during our next session, "when you were lucky if you had a flat stone by a creek on which to wash your loin cloth, do you think any of this mattered? Needy, not needy. In love, not in love. These are modern creations. What mattered then was (1) water, (2) food, (3) shelter, (4) procreation, (5) laundry." He raised his fingers one by one, starting with the pinky. My laundry, the thumb, was toiling below in the laundromat. "One element of your neediness is simply your hard-wired urge to find a mate and pass on your genes before a lion eats you or your filthy-smocked rival clubs you to death. In this, it is more likely than not that you would have been a great success—that your line would be preserved. What we consider an infinite emptiness, an endless desire for reassurance, may also be seen as the proper survival mode, the guarantor of your genetic contribution to the species. Congratulations are due."

Maybe so, I thought, but is this guy doing me any good? I wanted to get back to the point, to the here and now, to the nature of love and lust in this soulless metropolis.

"But how do I recognize the signs of encroaching neediness? How do I *let go* of a woman before she lets go of me?" This was clearly the crux—cultivating the ability to disengage, to be bodily present but emotionally aloof, to be there yet in absentia. Oh, what a cruel world!

He seemed to want to say something immediately, but hesitated.

"You have a decent though risk-averse sense of fashion."

"I work downtown at a bank, a decent if risk-averse institution," I said.

"Do you wash and iron your own shirts?"

"Yes, but what does this have to do-"

"You would rather not pay for such a domestic service. At heart, you are frugal."

"I prefer the word 'cheap,' actually. I'm a cheap Jew."

"No need for facetiousness. This sort of self-deprecation is only going to add to your problems. From whom did you learn to iron?"

"My father, who learned how to iron from his father. My grandfather had a picture frame shop, and Pop was a court reporter, but they both insisted on good shirts and pressed slacks."

"So this is making some sense to me now. There is a steady progression—from small merchant to civil servant to you, banker. And the common denominator is the well-ironed shirt, the sartorial discipline. This domestic chore has been handed down through the male line. You have seen your father control his destiny, and a man in his t-shirt leaning over an ironing board is a powerful and iconic symbol for you, one of independence, fortitude and masculinity."

He thought for a moment.

"I am pleased to say that I have a plan for you. Next time you arrive at our laundromat to do laundry, I want you to leave your favorite shirt behind. It will not be easy."

"Leave a shirt behind?"

"It's a start. You understand the significance of the shirt?"

"Of course." I wasn't sure, actually. Was the shirt like the women I couldn't let go of but whom I would now, symbolically, be leaving behind, or did it represent my father and the mindset and traditions I'd inherited from him? And a woman was not a shirt, by any means, just as she was not a pair of socks. And my father, bless him, is also not a shirt. I was a bit put off, honestly, but the doctor seemed assured that the exercise would do me good.

"But some of these shirts are expensive," I said.

"Excellent. They have monetary value as well. You must do as I say. Not just any shirt, but your favorite."

Next session I told him that down below, tumbling around with the rest of my laundry, was a beautiful ecru custom-made Sea Island cotton shirt. "Was at least 300 dollars," I said, "but when I wear it I feel like a million bucks."

"When you are done here you will dry what needs to be dried, but leave your special shirt in the washer."

"But what if someone sees I've left it behind? Someone will notice and probably just hand it to me."

"That won't happen."

"How do you know?"

"Because I will assist you by taking the shirt from the washing machine."

The laundromat is fluorescent-lit, has white linoleum tiles on the floor, a white drop ceiling, and hanging ferns above all the washers. It was a pretty busy night, with lots of East Villagers parading in with bags over their shoulders or pushing granny carts stuffed with dirty clothes. Some people would stroll right past all the washers and dryers to the drop-off counter in the back.

I put my clothing in two dryers and put what shouldn't be dried back into my laundry bag. Through the glass front of the laundromat I could see portions of pre-fab houses on wide-load tractor trailers going down Second Avenue in a convoy at about fifteen miles per hour. I sat down on one of the chairs and waited for my stuff to dry. I'd decided not to go through with it, the leaving-of-the-shirt-behind exercise, and I'd thought better of booking any more sessions with Lowencross and his endless spin cycle of ideas. My self-diagnosis was simple: I am a restless soul; And the cure: I am ready to embrace my imperfections! seemed just the remedy I was looking for.

In about ten minutes the Doc himself came down, looking a little pinched. I saw him peek into the first few washing machines in search of my shirt. Then he saw me and raised his eyebrows. We were on a mission after all. I shook my head in the negative and raised my laundry bag, indicating the shirt was within. He sat down next to me.

"I'm done," I said. "Thank you for your services. Just send me a bill for the outstanding balance."

"We are not even halfway through your cure," he whispered, looking around the place with suspicion.

"I appreciate it, but I don't think your methods are doing me any good."

"You are making an error of judgment, which does not surprise me. We are at a critical juncture and you have understandably lost your nerve. You've taken the load out before it's clean; you've washed with cold when you should have washed with hot; you've—"

"You're welcome to your opinion, naturally."

"Are you sure about this?" he said. Then, suddenly, "No no, it is my professional responsibility to persuade you to continue the treatment." He took my hand gently. "I will not release you."

"You will," I said, pulling my hand from his and then patting him on the back. "It'll be fine," I said. "If I feel the need for future sessions, I know where to find you, Doc. Now get out of here." And so he did, looking at me over his shoulder one last time with those wide-set eyes, and then pulling a small pad from his breast pocket and jotting something down.

Had I made a mistake? There I sat watching the washers and dryers, mulling over my situation, getting depressed. I was about to go back upstairs to Lowencross and ask for forgiveness when a young woman walked into the laundromat dragging a paisley laundry bag behind her. She was slim with long, curly black hair and thick eyebrows and chapped, full lips. She could have been Semitic, Italian, Latin American, I wasn't sure. She was wearing a long skirt and boots, and a kind of retro woven jacket from which beaded tassel after beaded tassel swung every which way as she moved. She honed in on the triple-loader in front of me and began throwing her laundry in. I felt an incandescent glow rise to my face. I couldn't take my eyes off of her. The sweet, musky odor of her laundry drifted my way and I felt embarrassed and excited.

She turned around and looked at me and I smiled. It felt indecent to keep watching so I looked at the floor between my feet. Then I got up, put another two quarters in the dryer to prolong my stay, and sat back down. I guessed this woman was in her late twenties or early thirties. Not a student and not a professional. Maybe an artist or trust-fund kid, though I'm often wrong on all counts with stuff like this. She finished loading the machine and fed it quarters. She hit the Start button and then sat down a couple of seats away. I looked at this woman, at the countless handles that proffered themselves from her garment.

"I'm Leonard," I said.

"That's nice," she said.

"And I love your jacket," I said.

"Do you?"

"I just said so. May I just touch it, briefly?"

"That's kind of a weird question."

"Here," and I lightly grasped one of the tassels with genuine love and pulled her toward me ever so lightly.

"What are you doing?" she said.

"Nothing," and I let go. "But listen, we've both got some time to kill so how about we get some coffee or something?"

"I don't think so. I'm planning on sitting right here," and she began digging through her purse so as to disengage me.

"Understood," I said. "Then let me get us something. There's a coffee place down the block. Can I get you a coffee? Chai? Hot chocolate?"

"Really. I don't know."

"It's simple. You let me deliver to you the beverage of your choice and you don't have to say another word. It ends there."

"Can you get me a latte?"

"I'd love to."

"With soy milk but almost no foam. Like maybe a tenth of an inch of foam. And a flat lid, not a sip lid?"

"Sure thing," I said, and out I went, dreaming of those tassels.

Her name was Ladonna and it wasn't that night, nor anytime that week, but a month before I was able to embrace her in the manner of a lover, and another week or so until I was able to convince her to wear her wonderful woven jacket such that I could pull her toward me and she can step away, and I can pull her toward me again, and she can laugh with the sunlight streaming through my windows lighting up her downy invisible sideburns, and she can step back from me as if I'm a bear, and I can pull her into me again, and she can rally against me as I envelope her in my arms and, and she can push me off and run into the kitchen, where I can take her by the arm and pull her toward me again and she can kiss my neck and fall on the floor as if submitting and, having deceived me, run off into the corner and throw the very same tasseled jacket at me and cower and wait to be taken by me to the bed, and nearly suffocated by my embrace and made love to, and she can run off back to her little, tiny, itsy bitsy apartment and I'll be on her heels, saying how much I love her, and all because I do love her. I do I do I do.

Cheerleaders

"Stay together, girls. Shooting begins in fifteen minutes."

Coming out of the subway station this is all that Ray heard. Everywhere he saw girls in red jackets, pleated skirts; sneakers and knee socks; earmuffs. Ray stopped at his usual kiosk for a frosted cruller.

"They clean me out, these cheer leaders," the Armenian man said. "Everything is gone. Gone!"

The three or four delis he passed were overrun by cheerleaders, the counter men and cashiers hidden behind ponytails and baseball caps. Farther down the block, past the generator trucks and catering tables, he came upon a fruit stand.

"They take everything but bananas," the man said. "They were told not to eat bananas. Give people the wrong idea." Ray bought a bunch for a dollar twenty-five and pushed his way toward his office building.

They came from large states, these cheerleaders. Far away states. They had perfect teeth, wore lip gloss, and held plastic pompoms, all of which glinted in the sunlight. A few of them were heavier than he thought they ought to be, and others had splotchy complexions (it was a cold morning). Down the block, he could see the glass lobby of his building. The security guards stood behind the glass, their gazes cast out upon the teenagers. An impossibly dense landscape of them lay between him and safety.

"Girls, we are shooting in ten minutes."

The audio must have had more than one source. He looked around for speaker stands or men on truck roofs with bullhorns, but he saw only girls in green windbreakers with high school logos, or crimson jackets with the image of a coyote. Rah rah rah, they were everywhere, crowding around him, hungry. A police sergeant in the Equine Division was standing in front of his fidgeting horse, the reins in one hand, the other shielding his eyes from the sun. "Goddamn," Ray heard him say. "Goddamn this town."

More of them were now crossing the wide avenue. About twenty of them came out of the Hilton wearing teal parkas with silhouettes of cheering boys and girls embroidered on their backs: two boys throwing a somersaulting girl into the air, her pigtails splayed, her legs scissored. Traffic could move neither forward nor backward. Ray was making only slight progress toward his office. He dropped the bunch of bananas.

A group of large cheerleaders was pushing toward him, pushing, their elbows above the other girls' heads. They were cheering in unison: "Let's go Eleolar High/You can get that pie in the sky!"

Ray took out his cell phone and called his wife. "Leslie? Something terrible is happening," he said. He could only hear her in digitized fragments asking what, what's happening? "I don't know how to describe it, exactly . . ." Then he lost the connection.

He saw that these were not taller girls, but girls stacked on girls, carried on the shoulders of their teammates, and even those carrying the girls—stout and red-faced—were cheering, "Let's go Eleolar High/Smash 'em, bash 'em, make 'em cry . . ." He couldn't lower his elbows to get his cell phone back into his pocket, and he was being buffeted, pulled along in this sea, unable to breathe, urged in all directions by a hundred girlish hands.

"Shooting begins in t-minus five minutes and counting, girls. Please take your positions."

The cheerleaders were all moving up the great avenue in writhing, united expectation. Generators began to hum, sucking down Number 2 diesel fuel, and sun-like lights came on. Cranes lifted giant pompoms to hang over the avenue and cross streets. Workers rolled reflector blankets down the facades of buildings from the rooftops until the streets were blazing. Delis, restaurants, and hotel lobbies disgorged more and more cheerleaders clad in optimistic colors. Ray was no longer visible, even to himself. He was atomized, free of the physical realm, breathed in by the gigantic girls who were all about him. He was part sour breath, part minty breath, part paramour in the autumn morning. He was carried along with them as they gathered beneath the giant pompoms and lined up, elbow to elbow and toe to heel. "It's time girls. We're shooting in ten seconds, nine, eight . . ."

The Cure

Rob's sitting at his local bar, a place called Dee Dee's on First Avenue and Fourth Street, when two women and a man, all in their thirties, come in and take up the stools next to him, leaving an empty one to his right. They order a bottle of Rioja and throw their jackets on the stool between him and their group without asking if he is saving it for someone. He isn't, but is it so obvious that he's alone?

"Last night," one of the women says to her friends, "I had this nightmare that I was raped by Darth Vader and his cock was *huge*." She puts her wine glass down and indicates the size of his penis. She's dressed in various shades of black and speaks with an accent, and she's tall. "Then, next thing I know, I'm giving birth to all these little tiny Darth Vaders and they all have little black helmets and capes, but they're also very wet from being inside of me, in my womb. Suddenly I'm not scared anymore and think how sad they all look, so wet from my insides. When I woke up I laughed. It *is* funny, right? No, I don't want to know what you think it means."

She looks over at Rob and smiles, momentarily including him in her group since, after all, he's right there. Her teeth are imperfect, chipped, one discolored. With those teeth and her accent, he imagines her in an Eastern European ghetto somewhere, a tough and desperate woman who does what she must to survive. That accent—he can't identify it definitively. Could be Czech or just as easily something different.

The second woman, an American who seems to be the girlfriend of the guy, says to the tall woman: "Jimmy was telling me about your extra, um, things . . ."

"Jimmy, why'd you tell her?" Then to the American woman: "I am not ashamed. Would you like to see them?"

"Very much," says the woman. She holds onto Jimmy's arm as if something terrible might happen.

The tall woman pulls the right short sleeve of her blouse down just beneath the armpit. "And there's one on the other side . . ." and she does the same on that side, where Rob catches a glimpse of her small defect. "I have four, just like my mommy and grandma. I'm worried that when I have children these extra ones will swell with milk for my baby Darth Vaders."

Contrasted against her pale skin, her black hair, eyebrows and irises give her an almost cartoon-like set of facial expressions. Rob notices her every eyebrow twitch and broken-toothed smile but doesn't know what any of them really mean. Her lips are large and uniformly rose-colored, like an odd-looking piece of fruit. And the sight of that extra nipple, pink and no areola, put a little bead of sweat on his upper lip.

As he looks away, a bit embarrassed at having stared at her, he thinks he sees her turn her head toward him.

The bartender, Daye, has red hair pulled back severely and braided. Her pale scalp shows through in zigzags and there's nothing to frame her diminutive, freckled face. She is pretty, and Rob knows she is kind, but he also knows for a fact that a baseball bat is hidden behind the bar and that she wouldn't hesitate to use it if things ever got out of hand. He loves that about Daye and he's always felt safe around her. She has also seen the stranger's little nipple and appears to be fascinated. It seems, suddenly, that a strange sexual voltage is running up and down the bar.

"I'd like to buy her a drink," Rob says to Daye.

Then he turns and puts his request to the foreign woman directly. "I'd like to buy you a drink. That's quite a show you put on—I couldn't help noticing."

She looks at him, puzzled, as if he's spoken too quickly for her to understand. "No, please don't buy me a drink," she says after waiting just long enough to make him certain of the answer. "But thank you for the kind offer." She turns back to her friends. "I am trying to meet a man with four hands," and they all laugh and Rob finishes his beer and orders another from Daye, who is blushing in sympathy for him.

"That's something, isn't it?" Rob says to her. "Four."

She draws the pint and doesn't say anything. Rob's been coming here for a long time, and it used to be that he would take a stool, have a beer, and his wife, Angie, would soon arrive.

Daye wipes down the bar in front of him, places the beer before him, and then leans in, turning her back to the threesome at his side. He knows what's coming.

"Hope you don't mind my bringing it up," she says, "but I saw your daughter yesterday with her little play group at Tompkins Square Park. How's she doing?"

"She still misses her mother. She's stubborn, still doesn't quite accept it."

"And you?"

"The only thing that's still screwing me up is insomnia. 'Give it time,' my shrink says, which is what he says about everything. I've seen him in here, by the way. Schackter, Ben Schackter's his name. Balding guy, built like a robot, drinks gimlets."

"You mean Benny?" she says, walking to the far end of the bar, "*this* Benny?" and she flicks the bar towel at an opened newspaper, a sort of bluff behind which Rob's mental healthcare practitioner has been absorbed in the sports section. He peers out now. With his perfectly round face and closely shaved dome, he gives the impression of an unerring creature. He smiles, lifts his small glass to Rob in silent tribute, and then raises the newspaper to cover his face once again.

"Shit," Rob says, "I told him I was gonna spend more time with Denise and less time, well, here." He takes a look over his shoulder at the group of people, and at the woman again. After a short pause he continues. "Anyway, I was saying that insomnia's still got its goddamn claws in me. And the bedroom is a little strange because Angie's scent is finally gone. I mean entirely gone. For a while I'd been sprinkling her perfume around." He takes a gulp of beer. "Which reminds me of why I came here tonight in the first place."

With a clinking sound, he lifts a cloth sack from between his feet and places it on the bar. Then he begins to remove bottles of perfume, lining them up on the urethaned surface.

"This morning I thought, it's really time to start clearing her things out. It's been two years."

"Has it been that long?" Daye says. "Jesus." She eyes the perfumes. "These look expensive."

"Yeah," he says. "She was a connoisseur of fine fragrances."

She grabs a small rococo bottle, opens it, and holds it to her nose. "What about this one?"

"She got it in Paris on a business trip."

"Smells like oranges, but not. I mean, it's also a bit musky. It's really sexy though. Oh god, I'm sorry for that. How can you stand it?"

"For a while I was smelling these every morning," he says. "Like I said, I'd even sprinkle the sheets with them. The doc over there will tell you that it's not a good thing to do, healing-wise. I have to let her go entirely. So . . . these should be worn by someone and what I'm saying is, Angie would want you to have them. We didn't have a lot of friends, and she always said how much she admired you. To be honest, I think she had a crush on you."

Daye is silent for a few seconds. She seems angry when she speaks.

"Don't take it wrong, but it's a bit creepy. I mean, I loved Angie. Seeing you two come in here together put a smile on my face. The Happy Couple, you know. And it's generous of you to think of me, but there's no way I can take these."

"Why not?"

"She's gone, sweetie. She's not coming back. Ever. Do you really want to come in here and be reminded of her whenever I wear this stuff?"

"That doesn't bother me." Robert leans in so that their faces are only a few inches apart. "I think you don't want to be reminded of death. But these, these should remind you of life."

"It's just too weird for me. Someone else will love them. Try them out on this one," she says, eyeing the woman who's still holding court with her two friends.

"Not a chance," he says, putting the bottles back into the sack.

"To tell you the truth, I'm not sure I like this trio that much anyway," Daye says, obviously wanting to change the topic. "They're all so goddamned self-assured."

"Maybe," he says, "but this one seems like she could suck the sorrow right out of my bones. I mean, look at those fucking lips."

"I'll call Benny over here cause you seem to be having some kind of breakthrough."

"Don't bother. I've got to get back to my girl. The sitter's probably wondering where the hell I am."

Out on the street Rob drops the sack of perfume bottles into a wire mesh garbage pail. Some of the bottles break and for a second the strong scents of his previous life overtake him and he stops dead in his tracks.

The following Wednesday night he stops in at DeeDee's, this time with his daughter, Denise, who he sets up with an electronic game and a Coke at the stool next to him. He asks Daye if she's seen the woman from the other night.

"She came by Sunday and sat there in the corner. Drained a bottle of wine on her own. But I did a little work for you. Her name's Clarissa and she's Finnish. She lives out in Red Hook." She hands him his pint. "She seems like a nutcase or something, though. Maybe just right for you."

About a week later he's cooking a chicken stir-fry for himself and his daughter when the phone rings. It's Daye. "I'm not sure it's a good thing I'm calling, but she's here." When Rob asks who, she says, "You know, your girl in black. So, you gonna come down before she's gone? She's alone smoldering in the corner."

He seats his daughter in front of her favorite video. "I'm going out for a little while. Eat your dinner."

"But what about yours?" she says.

"I'll have it when I get back."

"It's got chicken in it."

"Yes—and?"

"If you wait to eat it you might get salmonella."

"That's only before it's cooked. And people get hysterical. Look here, I'm covering it. I'm putting it in the fridge."

He looks up the number for DeeDee's in the phone book and puts a slip of paper in his daughter's hand. "Call me at the bar if something comes up."

"Like what?"

"Like anything. Call if anything at all comes up. I'm seven blocks away but daddy's as fast as the wind on his feet. Now watch the movie. The hawk's about to rescue the rat."

"It's an eagle," she says, "and a baby capybara. Later the grown-up capybara rescues the eagle."

Soon he's at DeeDee's and Daye is drawing a pint of his favorite lager. He sees the woman at the far end of the bar. She's folding her napkin into a tiny pyramid and trying to balance it on the edge of the ashtray. She looks at Rob and smiles.

He goes over and stands beside her with his beer and asks her why she's alone.

"I'm not allowed to be alone?" she says.

"Of course it's allowed, you just don't seem the type."

He sits on the stool next to her.

Within a few minutes he's leaning in to hear her speak. She speaks softly, choosing her words carefully. It makes no sense to him, the warm reception he's getting now, but after a couple of more pints he doesn't question it.

"Do you see how pretty Daye is, smoking one of my Dunhills," she says. "They're very expensive," and she draws hard on her own. "I know about you. Daye explained how you lost your wife in an automobile accident."

"Yes, it was a terrible, terrible thing to go through. But now I'm doing okay, actually."

"Oh yes? And that's why you left your girl at home while you come out to drink—to meet ladies?"

"I'm only human," he says. "No more and no less."

She takes his hand and circles her thumb on his palm. It reminds him of a school bus caught in a cul-de-sac. "You think your little girl will turn out well, don't you? But when the time comes, she'll seek out men like you—sad and alone, who keep their love crated in their souls. They believe that love can never be regained. To find it again would betray their dead lovers."

"You're fucking morose," Robert says, unsure how seriously to take her.

"And you're decent looking," she says as she leans against him. Her breath is heavy with the smell of cigarettes and wine and reminds him of high school, and college, and his first years in the city. His wife tried to quit smoking but never could. Before her, his girlfriends smoked. Every single one of them smoked and he never has. He breathes in the familiar breath.

"I've got a little girl to get back to."

⋆ ⋆ ⋆

Rob sits in a recliner in Dr. Schackter's office. Sunlight streams down into the small room which is a half-story below the sidewalk. It's around lunchtime and children from the local parochial school are playing outside, their shouts filtering in through the high horizontal windows.

"The sex is outstanding," he says. "I mean she's good and I'm good and as only you know"—he thinks of his wife because she had also known—"things weren't always up to par in that arena. But this one I've met, it's like I'm not me."

"I usually tell people in your state to be patient. However, in your situation things seem to be falling nicely into place. I imagine you have some lingering guilt about beginning a new sexual relationship."

"None," Robert responds. "At least I don't think so. Should I feel guilty about *that*?"

"Not necessarily. You seem fevered with this . . . what was her name—Clarissa?"

"Yeah, that's right," but Rob doesn't remember mentioning her name to the doctor.

When he gets home from his session he finds Clarissa and his daughter sitting on the living room chaise looking at his photo album. Clarissa is holding a picture of him as a ten year old presenting his mother with a chrysanthemum from her garden. Of all the pictures, he thinks. "How is our friend, the good doctor?" she says, standing up and kissing him. "Has he told you that I am your cure?"

"No, he hasn't exactly said that. It's good that I'm involved though, but I'm to take it slowly."

"I brought some things over," she says, pointing to her backpack on the floor. "It'll make it easier for me to stay over and no rushing back to Brooklyn for trifles all the time."

"Well, I guess it's good for you to have some stuff here," he says. He looks at her backpack on the floor. Some of her long hairs are caught in the zipper.

A few Sundays later, Rob, blasting Miles Davis and standing on a high ladder, patches a small hole in the bedroom ceiling. Clarissa stands below him and places a hand on one of his bare feet as he concentrates on spackling. He almost leaps off the ladder when she touches him.

"Are you out of your mind?" He catches his breath. "Make some fucking noise before you do that. I had no idea you were even here."

She hones in on the object of his work, a perfect circle the size of a dime, the outline of which is still visible through the wet spackle. "I've seen holes like that before," she says. "Deep holes. Did you buy a hook strong enough to hold a man? Did you account for the torque caused by a swinging mass?"

He hesitates, looking down at her from the ladder, her smile no different than usual, which is to say wide, imperfect, entirely non-revelatory. And what the hell did she say about torque? Is she an engineer now?

"You have no idea how it was at first without Angie around. I thought about it, you know, but I don't think I'd ever actually do it. Just drilling the hole. I mean it took me an hour to find the goddamn joist. That alone almost killed me. And I couldn't get over the idea that Denise might be the one that ended up finding the body. I know it doesn't make a whole lot of sense." He drops his voice. "Where is she, by the way? I don't want her to know a thing about this. Do you understand? Not a peep out of you."

"I picked her up from the park on my way here. She's washing up and then we'll dice vegetables for my vichyssoise."

Rob steps down from the ladder and sits on one of its rungs. "Listen, Clarissa, how did you know about that?" pointing to the ceiling. "Nobody knows about it except my shrink." He pauses and drops his head. "You've arranged this—meeting me," he says quietly, as if nobody else were in the room. "This whole thing has been arranged. Yes yes, that would explain some things." When he looks back at her, his eyes are red-rimmed.

She takes his hands in hers. "I am an expensive drug cocktail, so your insurance company believes. But I can stay here for a long time," she says. "I can stay here forever if that's what you need."

"Hey why not, right? I mean hell," he says, reddening, "let's commit fraud and enjoy ourselves. Whose bright idea was it?"

"The bartender's," she says. "And then your doctor's too. They said you needed help and, well, I needed something too."

"The money."

"And a place to live, and maybe a green card down the road. But now I like you too."

"I don't want you around my daughter."

"That's nonsense. I'm harmless. And with you she'll never learn how to cook."

"And Schackter agreed to all this?"

"He did the paperwork with the insurance company. He somehow gets reimbursement—for extra sessions and drugs or something, and then writes me a check."

"And what does he get out of it?"

"His patient gets better and he has more time to see other patients."

"Does he get you too?"

"No, he doesn't get me. Only you get me."

"He'll go to hell."

"Why? You're happy, I'm happy, Denise is happy. 'Screw the big brother, the man.' I've heard you say that. Well that's what we're doing and it should feel . . . liberating."

"Look, the only kind of therapy this is going to be for me, from now on, is physical therapy. You understand what I'm saying?"

"What if I like it? You're such a gentle lover."

"Not anymore."

"You don't scare me, mister," and that night he was rough with her but it exhausted him and afterward he stood looking at himself under the flickering light in the bathroom mirror, at his own unsure eyes. He had never been capable of violence of any kind. As a kid he practically teared up whenever someone stamped out an insect. The few times Angie wanted to see what it would be like to be tied up by him, to be restrained, to be done until she couldn't breathe, as she put it, he couldn't do it. And he kept putting it off, eventually telling her the truth—that he couldn't bear to see her in that demeaned position. "Oh come *on*," she'd said, "I'm asking you to; just play the role. It'll be good for both of us."

He came out of the bathroom, got back into bed and pressed himself against Clarissa. She was as he'd left her, facing the outside of the bed, her back to him. As he lay down he could see her blinking, lost in thought.

He ran his fingers through her hair.

"One thing I hadn't realized," she said, "you have strong hands, hands like vises. Don't squeeze my arms so hard next time if you don't want me to show bruises," she said. "Or if you don't care one way or the other, do."

"I won't then," he said, still stroking her hair. "Will you turn around so I can see your face before I fall asleep?"

"No," she said, "but wake me up when you're ready to do it again. You don't scare me."

"Turn around," he said.

"I'll make you coffee in the morning," she said, and soon her breathing settled and he knew she was asleep.

Streetlights down below on Tenth Street were casting shadows of the Venetian blinds onto the ceiling over the bed. Murky parallel lines that were only ever affected in the summer, when moths circled the lights. But it was February now, the radiators creaked, his and Clarissa's body heat was building up under the duvet and soon he knew he'd be drifting off too. But the shadows—he and Angie had shared the view of those shadows for five years and neither had ever said a thing, and why should they have?

"Look at the shadows," he said now, trying to travel backward in time, hoping those words would transform the woman beside him into Angie, knowing there would be no response.

He began to drift off at last and imagined himself being lowered deep into the earth, far down, dropping into the dark warm embrace of the primal mother. Then he was moving toward the molten core, every square inch of his body compressed unbearably until he was no more than a thimbleful of inert matter, never to surface again.

Motel Girl

Behind the counter of the motel office a teenage girl was laboring with an antiquated adding machine, punching the numeric keys then cranking down a long handle causing the thing to caching loudly and advance the tattered roll of paper. She glanced at me caustically, continued her bookkeeping, had pimples in neat rows on either side of her nose. Black heads, white heads, purple scars from attempts at eradication. But the subtle lines of her face, the sultry lips pursed in concentration, her high cheekbones, large flitting blue eyes (slightly glazed over), all indicated a beauty that was stark and undernourished. I couldn't help staring for a second. Once those pimples ran their course, I thought, she'd be in high demand, a real knockout.

"Passing through or stayin' for a while?" she asked, turning her blank gaze back to the narrow strip of paper feeding into the machine.

"Just passing through. Thought I'd be able to drive straight on into the mountains. Front end alignment's off on the old beast though. Car pulls one way, you steer the other. You get tired fast driving like that."

"Sure," she said, keeping her energy focused on punching numbers into the machine. "It's thirty-four ninety-five plus tax for the night."

I paid cash, got my key, left the girl to her torturous accounting.

The shower in my room had one of those heads that swirled or pulsed the water and could make skin with my pallid hue the color of boiled ham. I put the thing on the coarsest setting and let it pulverize my back. I'd been hunched over all day, leaning forward in concentration, correcting the right-hand torsion of the steering wheel. After the shower, I wrapped myself in a towel and flopped onto the squeaky bed. Every time a car sped past the motel on the highway outside, a set of shadows from its headlights would crawl up the wall to the ceiling where they would stretch oblongly then crawl back down the other wall, as if the shadows were alive and had intent. I'd been seeing this pattern since I was a kid and was always comforted by it. These celestial creatures are cast upon our world, victims of light, angles, velocity.

Suddenly the dance was broken by a huge, oblique shadow passing across the wall. A knock at the door followed. I opened it a crack and peeked out. It was the veiled beauty, the pimpled desk girl. "I need to change your bedding," she said. She seemed somewhat less dour this time. Now, at least, a small smile appeared, although it seemed accidental, and vanished immediately. I put my jeans on and opened the door. "Sorry about this. I shoulda done it this morning."

She got right down to business, ripping off the old bedding, rolling it up and tossing it by the door and then just as energetically installing the new flat sheets and pillow cases. This all took a little while and I just watched, fingering my naval with my pinkie like I do when I'm deviously amused. Despite the piteous state of her complexion, she was, by the most male and superficial of standards, a sexually enchanting girl.

"What about the comforter, are you going to change that too?" I asked.

"No need. Just a couple of senior citizens in here before you. Doubt they could do damage."

"If possible, I'd like a clean one anyway. It seems a little mildewy."

"Why do you want a clean one when this one's clean? You mean you want a different clean one."

"It's just a matter of sanitary conditions. I'm a little nuts about these things. Blame it on my mother. She ran a tight ship."

The girl mumbled something underneath her breath while violently whipping up the pillows.

"If you're talking to me," I said in my least confrontational tone, "you can speak your mind. It's better not to hold things back."

"No offense, mister," she said, turning to me and bending to one side like an MTV-taught homegirl, hands on hips, neck hinged forward doubly, "but I don't need a freakin' social worker type up here from New York City trying to guide me to a better way of life."

"I'm not a social worker," I said, a little offended at the remark. "It's just that if you're pissed off, don't worry about letting it out. It might make you feel better."

This made perfect sense to me. She was young, trapped here under god knows what conditions and probably, I assured myself, could use someone like me to teach her how to best release tension. If they're not careful, sweet things like her turn into angry obese housewives living with manic, unemployed, alcoholic husbands in trailer parks. The clever ones get rich by burning the place down and suing the stove company, or the light bulb company, or any manufacturer that has product liability insurance. As an actuarial intern in college, I had catalogued some of these cases and was amazed at how good a living could be made out in the boonies by simply burning and suing. I'd been taught that when fatalities were involved, it was usually the real thing, in which case the settlement was always lower anyway.

I could see myself in the mirror over the headboard and I didn't like the expression on my face—amused condescension. I had no interest in trying to determine what was really going on with this young woman. Had I looked below the surface, I might have sensed the darkness, the real-life threat lurking beneath that blemished skin. All I knew was that I wanted a clean comforter, which at the time seemed both reasonable and necessary. Still, I was unable to keep my eyes off her slim body, virgin to cellulite, stray body hairs, and the inevitable post-adolescent spread. And that cute little body, I thought, would look even better in clothes that weren't ten years out of date. This thought—that her clothes were old, cheap, of the worst poly-nylon taste—elicited another grin, which I hoped she hadn't noticed. I was a real jackass, that's for sure, but for the time being, an amused one.

She held a corner of the comforter under her nose and gave it a quick whiff. She seemed satisfied. It did look perfectly clean, but you never know what kinds of microscopic monsters could be making a habitat—like herds of bison grazing the American grasslands—out of that comforter.

"You're not special, you know. I saw how you looked at me when you checked in. I see you lookin' me up and down now. You think I'm a hick. You think I'm a dumb teenager. What plans you got for me, anyway?"

What was this duplicity, saying all this while measuring me up with a seductive glare of her own, tempting me to test my abilities on her? I hadn't seen a look like that since high school and it was a look I didn't particularly miss. It said that she knew of the power she possessed: feminine youth in full blossom, petals unfurling, sweet balm erupting. Was I supposed to rise to this challenge? I said nothing in response to her question. At that moment I couldn't muster the moral armor I would need to strip a teenager of the last remnants of her childhood. Yet I couldn't help wondering how she would behave under my guidance. My wonderings gave way to vivid conjurings of this straggly, glum girl lying supine beneath me, whispering softly, amorously groaning in my ear. An embarrassing state of arousal set in.

She turned to look out the window. I could see her face reflected in the glass, the way its expression took on a hardness when confronting its own image. Putting a hand on the window to shield against the glare, to cancel her reflection, she stared into the darkness.

"It's begun to snow," she said.

Perhaps in a gesture of reconciliation, she directed me under her hand. Outside, tiny white flakes drifted down in dense, windless sheets. "We're supposed to get two feet," she said. "Guess you didn't listen to the weather, huh."

She gathered up the old sheets and turned to me, hugging the large bundle to her chest. "You might be trapped here for a few days. Hope you got enough cash for the room." She opened the door to leave.

"Thanks for everything," I said.

"I'll be back later with a clean comforter."

The door clicked behind her and then all was dead silent, and even more so. I turned the lights off and watched the snow fall. At the far end of the motel parking lot fir trees rose, dark and shadow-like, toward the moon, around which a barely discernible corona of light broke through the haze of snow. With this burgeoning blizzard the shadow-play on the walls ceased, and along with it the sense of motion I'd had, that it was the room itself gliding down the highway, passing stationary lights. Yet light was filtering in somehow, the bright eerie quality of which would make you think you were seeing in the dark by some special power. Sitting on the bed, I became very calm, feeling insulated by the storm, by the silence, and knowing that even in broad daylight my field of vision would be limited. I thought: I will not contemplate anything beyond the physical bounds of my sight. With my feet on the floor and my back, still aching and unsprung against the comforter, I fell asleep.

Hazy-headed, I rose from bed and looked at my watch. It was one in the morning. I was pretty sure someone had been knocking on the door for a while. The room was freezing. No heat rose from the radiator, no hiss of steam or creaking of electrical elements gave even the illusion of warmth. I opened the door and there stood the motel girl, a dusting of snow on her dirty blond hair. I turned the lights on. She stepped in, a blast of cold squeezing through with her.

She had changed her clothing, was wearing jeans, an olive-colored t-shirt with a low V. The clothing fit her snugly, revealing the intimate contours of her inner thighs and narrow ass, her nascent breasts, and the smooth bridge of her clavicles. In a year or two, I said to myself, her bodily presence would turn every head in any bar and cause most men to growl, blush, or grin helplessly, like adolescents. As if that weren't enough, she was shivering like a helpless and lost orphan, face flushed with cold—why hadn't she worn a jacket?—teeth chattering. Oh, I was bad. Her acne could be overlooked. It even added to the image of a dejected, do-anything teenage girl who has nothing to lose, not even her innocence. She held the neatly folded comforter, an ugly plaid flannel, at about the level of her breasts.

"If you'd be kind enough to fold up the one on your bed, I'll lay this one out for you."

Doing as requested, I unruffled the old comforter and began to fold it. She leaned over me, watching. Her breath, warm and moist in the cold air, tickled the hairs on the back of my neck. I folded the comforter into precise halves, fourths, eighths, sixteenths, continuing the equation in my head in order to distract myself from her presence: two to the nth power equals thirty-two when n equals five, sixty-four when n equals six, one-twenty-eight when n equals seven . . . .

"I saw you lookin' at me just now and I bet I know what you're thinking. You're thinking 'I bet she's a good, tight, fuck.' Am I right? Don't think I don't know that look," she continued. "I've seen it in half the truckers and salesmen who've passed through this damn place. You think I'm a naïve thing for your taking, don't you?"

She was wearing sparkly eye shadow, had made herself up for this.

I put the folded comforter on the floor.

"I have no idea where you get your ideas but I think I've heard enough of them."

"Actually, I feel kinda sorry for guys like you. It must be hard at your age. All you wanna do is screw screw screw anything that won't talk back: 'Oh you're the master, you're the king. No one does it like *you*.' Some little hick slut would be a lot of fun, wouldn't she? You'd feel good taking pity on her. 'Poor girl,' you'd say, 'miserable face.'"

I hesitated. Was this simply the manifestation of a hormonal imbalance, of whatever had set in motion the strange symmetry of her skin affliction? Or could it be a reaction against overwhelming responsibility? After all, she seemed to be running the entire motel by herself. Or maybe some combination of the two made the most sense.

"Listen to me, you are not ugly in the least. Saying that about yourself, that kind of self-effacement, is only going to make things more difficult. The truth is you're actually quite pretty." Pretty. That's not what she wants to hear. A girl is pretty, a woman is what? "When that acne clears up you'll have the face of a model. And I mean a supermodel, as in one word, paparazzi around every corner, focus of every guy's fantasies. Never a dull minute. I mean it all. Now why don't you leave me the comforter, then we can both get some sleep?"

She took a step toward me and stood like a pugilist.

"I've had a hard time with guys like you. Maybe you think you're a little kinder than some of the others, but you still got that look that says you'll drug me then fuck me. Or maybe you'll just punch me out first."

Suddenly I had the urge to comfort her, to run her tangled hair between my fingers, to lightly pass my lips over her pocked face. But what would she think I was doing? And all at once the urgency I'd felt to seduce her vanished. Had I been a young father, this girl could be my daughter.

"Please let me alone to sleep," I said at last, now completely awake and a little sore about it. I held my arms out. "May I have the comforter?"

"Of course," she sighed, looking down at her feet. "I'm sorry for all this." I lifted the clean comforter from her outstretched arms and threw it on the bed. Beneath it she had been holding a pistol that she was now pointing at my chest. She was still, completely calm, and seemingly at peace.

"Do you know that it's physio—oh, what's the word? Yes, physiologically—do you know that it's physiologically impossible for a woman, or in my case, girl," she added demurely, "to rape a man? If you don't want to be fucked by me, then you can't be fucked by me. Maybe if women could rape men, they'd be doing it all the time, same as you do to us."

Though her voice had gone dead cold, there was a glimmer in her eyes that said she was enjoying herself, that she was getting off. "At least try to put a smile on your cute little face," she said.

I stammered, trying but unable to stave off a nervous grin. After all, this couldn't really be happening. "What the hell are you doing? I don't need this."

"That's understandable. Now come closer my little growed up man." She giggled like a schoolgirl about to kiss a boy for the first time.

Outside, the wind had picked up and was whipping against the windows, which were rattling in their frames. The place was creaking like a ship and somewhere an acoustic anomaly—loose siding or fascia, a gutter downspout—was catching the wind and broadcasting an endless flute sound that was not unpleasant.

Hesitantly, I stepped forward, and could see sweat glistening around her lips despite the cold. Her neck and chest had turned crimson as if from a sexual flush; her cheeks were pink beneath the flesh's lunar surface. She raised the pistol, a .45, to my face. The barrel was by no means small.

"Open your mouth for my gun," she said, her voice throaty. "Come on sweetie pie, open your mouth."

"No. I won't."

"Do you want me to take you to where the lights don't shine?" She cocked the gun. "BANG!" She held the cold steel tip to my lips. I opened my mouth, but only a little. "C'mon, got to open wider if you don't want your teeth to get chipped. I don't plan on being so gentle. Yes. That's good. Boy, you've got such a nice tongue. Now don't fight me with it, keep it tucked away."

She slowly pushed the gun into my mouth then pulled it out, saw that it was dry, spat on it, and thrust it in again.

"Gosh, I wish this thing had nerves!"

With one hand she held the pistol tightly, her trigger finger securely in its place, and with the other she held the back of my head. Using her arm she forcefully thrust the gun into my throat. I could taste blood drawn by the front sight. I could barely get air in and out through my nose. She moved her hand from my neck down to my pants, over my groin.

"How sad," she said, tightening her grip. "Hope this doesn't become a condition for you. These things can last for years."

Saliva and blood were dripping down my chin. My legs were weak and about to give way when the thrusting became so furious that I was sure, intentional or not, this girl would shoot me dead. I managed to briefly escape the confines of my body and float above an autumnal countryside, but she brought me back, saying that it was almost over. She shone with sweat, her huge pupils emanating a calm animal savagery. I was suffocating and nearly unconscious. In the end there was the empty metallic click of the hammer. Her eyes fluttered, rolled back, and a few spasms shook her.

At last she removed the pistol from my mouth.

"Shoot," she said, panting, regaining her composure, "I'm not gonna wash this gun for a while. It's good and sticky."

I took a delirious, pathetic swing at her, but she blocked it and then pistol-whipped me. After that I was gone, a floating head, a pain-filled balloon, watching from above as she lifted my feet off the floor and rolled my limp body onto the bed.

* * *

For a few seconds, sitting up in my stiffened clothing, my breath rising in a cloud, I forgot where I was, what had occurred. I got out of bed and rubbed the thin gloss of ice from the inside of the window, but snow had quaintly frosted the outside. I gave the glass a hard tap and it fell away from its muntin, landing inaudibly in the snow outside. Light and freezing air poured in. The sky was a cloudless blue. In the parking lot a vortex of wind was sweeping snow, like dust, off the roof of my old AMC Hornet.

I made my way into the bathroom, my bones rattling with cold. In the flaking mirror over the sink, I saw that my lips were swollen and raw, but not torn up as badly as they were beginning to feel. Swallowing was excruciating. The wound issued by the butt of the pistol was about an inch in length and was raised in such a perfectly smooth and symmetrical fashion that it made my stomach turn. The hair surrounding the wound was matted with blood. I cleaned the sticky gash with a washcloth and cold water, put on an oxford, and collected my things.

As I was warming up the car and scraping ice off the windshield, I noticed that the motel looked worse than I had recalled. Much worse. I'd arrived in darkness so hadn't seen the broken windows or the badly faded vinyl siding that was hanging from the exterior in long strips. A few of the windows were boarded up and an old interstate sign was nailed over the entrance to one room, sealing it. A large arrow that had probably guided a million drivers to some connecting capillary of a road now pointed downward into the snow, the route number showing only a leading three. I got into my car and revved the engine until the heat kicked on and began to defrost the windshield.

The tires spun wildly at first, but eventually they dug in. I made my way toward the motel office, slowly picking up speed. The old Hornet, straight six straining at full throttle, tires singing in a spray of icy froth, steering wheel pulling right, entered the motel office through the south-facing wall. Glass, particle board, pine paneling, two-by-fours all exploded with the impact. The front desk and other furnishings were obliterated in a hail of splinters before the car came to rest. Glass crunched beneath my feet as I got out.

The place was empty, the motel girl nowhere to be seen. The ancient adding machine had been catapulted across the office and there had taken a fair bite out of the drywall. Still caught in its steel teeth was the strip of paper on which the figures of her previous night's labors were indelibly etched. I pulled it out. It contained nonsense, random numbers in long strings. About twenty lines of them.

I went to each room in the motel, starting with the small one behind the office. With the exception of the one I had spent my night in, they all seemed to have been empty for years.

It was a beautiful morning, clear and brisk. I backed the car out of the demolished office and spat some blood into the snow. As I drove out of there I kept the windows open to let in the freezing air, which killed some of the pain. The sky was a Caribbean blue, that of a coral atoll giving way to the deep. I had to drive slowly in the snow as the tires on the old beast were not the greatest.

The Sweater

Anna sat in the darkest corner of the park in the middle of the night, knitting. Even though she could see cars going down the lighted avenue and sometimes couples crossing from one side of the park to the other, when she looked down she could only decipher the outline of her arms and fingers, and the sweater was like an emerging shadow. At first it had been the size of a napkin, but it was beginning to grow. She had a vague sense of it and she kept thinking of her father as she knitted, which was the point. Her father was a few blocks away, lying on a big bed in a stuffy room with a nurse sitting outside of his door. Anna had snuck out when things quieted down in the house. It was the middle of June, 1960, and she was in Stuyvesant Square Park in Manhattan.

Two men were smoking a few benches away, and she could tell they didn't know what she was doing. She figured they could hear the tacking sounds of the knitting needles even though she tried to keep it quiet. For some reason she wasn't scared. If her father knew she were there, in such blackness, in the darkest of dark folds, so late at night, he would have gotten out of bed, as sick as he was, and dragged her home. She could imagine him, wheezing, swollen-ankled in his bathrobe. Flashlight in one hand, the other gripping a pistol. When she looked over at the smokers she could see the red ember of their cigarette moving between their faces, illuminating their eyes and eyebrows, the contours of their noses.

Then a young woman or girl who was wearing a strong perfume sat down at the opposite end of Anna's bench. As if there were no empty benches anywhere in the park. Anna saw the figure approach as you might see a blob under your closed eyelids grow larger and take on some kind of definitive form—an iron, a hat, a person walking daintily. The bench creaked, the back deformed slightly as the girl sat down on the other end.

After a few minutes of sitting still, so still that she disappeared into the darkness, this perfumed person said, as if they'd been in the throes of a conversation, "You wouldn't believe the things my brother wants me to do for him and his friends." Her voice sounded like that of a well-educated girl who hoped to inherit the world. This, Anna supposed, is what happens when you venture out late at night on your own. Having never done so before, she now could see that with darkness came adventure and a certain unexpected strangeness. She stopped her knitting and looked at the shadow at the other end of the bench, saying nothing, not even exhaling.

"I'm sorry," the girl said, "It's rude of me to interrupt like that. My name's Arabelle. If you don't mind, may I ask what you're doing there?"

"I'm knitting a sweater," Anna said.

"In the dark?"

"What does it look like to you?"

"May I feel it?"

The girl moved closer to her and her hand wandered lightly over Anna's body until it came to the object in her lap. Anna froze at the stranger's hand, though it was warm and well-behaved. "Oh, that's really soft. I don't know anything about knitting, but it feels like you're using fine yarn."

"The finest. It's from Scotland. I want the sweater to be extra comfortable for my father. He's very sick."

"I know."

"You know?"

"Yes, and I'm sorry. But at least your father's been there for you. I live with my mother and my great uncle. My father ran off with the Negro maid when my mother was pregnant with me."

"That must be difficult."

"It's only my brother and his friends that are difficult. The brats. They stole some of my underthings last week, and tonight they broke into the bathroom while I was in the shower."

"Oh my, I see."

"It's no way to live for a girl like me. Which is why I'm going to run away to Jones Beach. I'll live there for a few days—right on the beach. Can you imagine that?"

"I don't mean to be rude, but I have to finish this sweater."

"The very soft sweater."

Anna started knitting again and then immediately stopped.

"I'm sorry, but I don't understand something you said. Did you know my father was ill?"

"I guessed it. I have this sort of extraordinary way of seeing people. When it's this dark I can pick out troubled people by these little sparks coming out of their scalps. If it's winter and they're wearing hats I can't see anything. But otherwise little blue sparks. So when you mentioned your father, I realized that that must be it, since it looked to me like you were putting out some sparks, at least from a distance."

Anna let go of her knitting and tentatively touched the top of her head.

"I'm not always right. I'm about sixty:forty, right to wrong," Arabelle said. "Sometimes I tell people they're troubled and they look like they're going to smack me. Who's this little negra girl anyway? they wonder. I can see the rage boiling up in them and that's how I know I'm wrong."

"I didn't know you're a Negro."

"Black as the night."

"But your father. You said your father ran off with the Negro maid?"

"Yes. He ran off with the Negro maid."

Anna had stopped knitting the sweater several times to talk to the girl and now wasn't sure if she was at the armpit or the shoulder of the first sleeve but she thought it was the armpit and picked it up from there. The men who were smoking had moved to a closer bench. They were whispering to each other in a way that showed they wanted to be heard whispering to each other. Befinned cars glided down Second Avenue. A policeman on foot patrol passed by the far end of the park, raking his nightstick along the wrought iron fence. Anna had been hearing that sound from a distance for years because in the summer she left her bedroom windows open. But this was the first time she actually saw it happening.

Arabelle moved closer. "These benches are sure not luxurious," she said. "Are you going to sleep here tonight?"

"No, I'm going to knit. That's all. I need to finish this sweater before the sun rises. I don't want to see what I'm doing."

"I'm beginning to understand."

"Do you really? I'm curious, how will you get to the beach?"

Anna found that by talking slowly and concentrating on what she was doing, she could simultaneously pay attention to the conversation and her knitting. She had set up a sweater map in her mind, and over that map was a grid, A1 through G7, and she could remember what rectangle she was in.

"I've got some cash and could take a taxi. Or maybe a Greyhound. Or I could hitchhike."

"Are you a pretty girl?" Anna asked. She didn't want a pretty girl, Negro or otherwise, out there on her own hitchhiking from Manhattan all the way out to Long Island. It was dangerous, and you never knew what kind of trouble the night could bring to a girl with such a sweet voice.

"Oh, I'm so-so. But don't worry. I wouldn't let just anyone pick me up. He'd have to be a gorgeous devil, I mean really smashingly beautiful. What about you—are you attractive?"

"I don't know anymore. I haven't looked at myself in the mirror like that for a long time. Since my father's been bed-ridden. They say his kidneys are failing." She was on rectangle B6.

"I'll bet you are pretty, though. May I touch your face?"

"No."

After that Arabelle moved back to the far end of the bench and didn't say anything for a while. The knitting accelerated and was as full of love as possible. Anna kept the image of her father in the front of all her other thoughts. Any other thoughts, and even the thoughts she was having while talking to the Negro girl, were filtered through the translucent movie images of her father and everything she could recount about their life together.

The two people who had been smoking were smoking again and it became apparent that they were smoking marijuana this time, not cigarettes. The smell drifted over the park bench and would be forever and minutely a part of the sweater. The smokers started talking loudly.

"I wonder what she's doing," one said.

Then the other: "Her hands are dueling. She's playing with something, man. What's all the clicking, that glimmer glimmer?"

"I wonder if she's *insane*."

"She's knitting," Arabelle said from the other end of the bench, "so leave her be."

They laughed after that, but not in an endearing way, and then in a little while they left. She was now about two-fifths of the way through the sweater, by her estimates. She would liked to have been able to work some geometric shapes into the sweater since her father had made his living as a mathematics teacher at a private school on the Upper West Side. But she knew her limitations.

"I think I'll sleep here next to you, if that's okay," Arabelle said out of the darkness. "They'll never find me." Just then a police car sped down Second Avenue, the single light spinning in a glass enclosure the shape and size of a fez. "See? I'll bet that's them looking for me. Poor Mom must be worried stiff."

In a little while the girl had taken up the fetal position on the bench and the top of her head was pressed lightly against Anna's left thigh. Her processed hair reflected distant lamp light. Her breathing was completely free and bordered on snoring. She must be lost in dreams, Anna thought. It was a relief, the silence.

Soon Anna forgot about the grid over the sweater map and she knitted without forethought, without knowing or caring where exactly she was. The sweater was taking on a larger meaning, something she had not expected but had hoped for nonetheless. Her father: she could never love him as much as he wished. Though he was always close by, either caressing her hair, telling her stories, standing over her with his burdensome, ballooned body as she did her homework, or even vetting the boys she dated—though he did all these things, she never felt able to give herself to him as he wished. It was as if he'd wanted her to crawl inside of him or to become his lover, though she wouldn't put it in exactly those terms. This sweater would make up that difference, would be the delta, as he always liked to say, between what she'd given him and what he desired.

She knitted, and she intermittently slept and dreamed, and in those dreams she continued to knit, and she dreamed a sweater, and she knit dreams, and the needles moved quickly. When the sun broke over Second Avenue the spools of thread were gone.

Arabelle was the first to wake. "Isn't that something marvelous!" she said.

Anna opened her eyes and saw her neighbor clearly for the first time. She had small, soft features and a round face. Yes, she was a Negro, but her hair was straighter than Anna's and her eyes were light in color, either green or hazel. Her chin had a tiny cleft the shape of a screwdriver tip.

Then Anna looked down at the sweater. It was like nothing she'd ever seen before. There was no guarantee that it could be worn by anyone. Arabelle leaned over and pressed her hand firmly into it, kneading it.

"What do we call it?"

"We don't call it anything," Anna said.

In the morning light the veil was lifted, the gauze of dreaminess gone without a trace. The first thing she reiterated in her own mind was that her father did not trust blacks, even young teenage girls. She believed, in a flash, that this young woman was trying to deceive her somehow. She could hear her father. "The little nigger girl wants to steal your purse." But her bag was still by her side. Searching it with her hand, she felt her keys and her purse; unclasping her purse, she felt the folds of cash. This runaway *was* a Negro, sure enough, but, yes, as the sun hit them, Anna could now see that she had piercing green eyes. Those eyes bespoke something profound and beautiful, something unearthly.

Arabelle's hand was now wrist-deep in the sweater, which seemed a physically impossible act. "It's the closest thing to love I've ever actually touched," she said.

"I'm going to take it home now," Anna said.

"Let me walk with you."

"My father is very ill so you won't be able to come inside. Not even into the lobby of the building."

"I understand how that works." She pressed her hand farther into the sweater until her arm had vanished up to her elbow. She closed her eyes. In about a minute she smiled and opened them.

"I think I've discovered something. Let me carry the sweater for you. I won't harm a loop."

Despite her best instincts, Anna allowed the girl to lift it off of her. She could feel the garment's imprint, the way it had lain on her lap like a sleeping baby. Her thighs were moist from sweat or condensation. They walked past a comatose bum several benches away and then past a fountain that seemed to be spouting bees but no water, and then they walked past a bed of impatiens. The flowers spilled onto the paving stones and seed pods burst as the girls' ankles brushed against them. They exited the park and continued west on East Sixteenth Street.

"Why are you looking at me like that?" Arabelle said.

"I'm not sure. I hadn't really thought about it. I hadn't really thought about the fact that. . ."

"Yes. I know. And your father is not the kindest man when it comes to the Negro race, now is he?"

"You know this?"

"I think you've knitted your memories of him into the sweater."

"Oh. But it's true. You could never set foot in our apartment. He keeps a pistol under his pillow. He's deathly serious about maintaining the racial divide."

Arabelle stopped walking and held the sweater to her chest. The two young women were now facing each other, Arabelle looking west and Anna looking east back toward the park.

"I think the sweater is for you, not him," Arabelle said. "I don't think he'll ever be able to wear it. Can you even tell me what it looks like?" She then held it up to her body, but the sweater wouldn't settle into any one shape. It seemed folded in upon itself in impossible configurations, though here and there hints of a real sweater could be deciphered—one long sleeve, a V for the neck, an edge of fabric.

"If you know all this about my father, why are you following me?" Anna could feel something welling up inside of her—rage, sorrow, a certainty that life would never be the same from this moment on. "Didn't you feel it?"

"What?"

"The hatred." She heard herself shouting now. "Didn't you feel the *hatred*, Arabelle?"

"Yes. I felt the hatred."

"You know what he would do to you, to me, if he saw us walk into his home together? Never. Never in my life have I been so close to a Negro. And here I am, having spent the night on a park bench with one, and a stranger at that. I can't even explain it to myself."

"No crime has been committed."

"Are you certain? I feel dirty, filthy, and I have no doubt that you've taken something from me. But for the life of me I can't figure out what."

"That's your father talking."

"My father loves me. He's the dearest man in this world. You don't know him."

"I know what you feel about him. And you just said yourself that–."

"Give me the sweater. Give it to me."

Anna lunged just as Arabelle threw the sweater toward her. It leapt into the air, its formlessness made more so as it tumbled over itself. Anna caught it before it hit the ground. She searched for a sleeve, a neck hole, anything. She held it to her chest, pressed it against her face, and then held it before her at arm's length. "I don't want this godforsaken thing anymore." She threw it down to the asphalt and turned back to see that the street was deserted. She heard a distant sound, the hard clop-clop of a woman's shoes on asphalt.

"Arabelle?"

Nothing.

She picked the sweater back up and walked west on Sixteenth Street toward her home. A hearse, shiny, black, the longest car she'd seen in a year, was coming down in the opposite direction. It pulled to the curb in front of her building and two black men dressed in white uniforms pulled a gurney out of the back of the vehicle. The chrome legs of the gurney clicked into place, the sound echoing down the block. It was still early, the sun just edging over the buildings to her east. Nobody seemed to be awake yet. A short white man with angular features got out of the driver's seat and started to give directions to the men. They pushed the gurney ahead of them as if it were the guest of honor, one of them holding the door of her building open for it. She followed them inside and was stopped by the concierge.

"Your father," he said. "I'm sorry."

"I thought so." She tried her best to hold back her tears. "May he be in heaven."

"Your mother was frantic last night. We searched all your usual hiding places. To have lost two, that would have meant the end for her, and so three would have left this earth."

"I was in the park, Mr. Miller. Now I want to see my father before they take him away."

"I'll call ahead to let your mother know. The doctor and nurse are there. I believe your mother is sedated, poor thing. What's that you're carrying?"

"A sweater."

"Is it now?"

"Yes. A memory sweater. It's a tradition. From Iceland, Mr. Miller. You knit a sweater for the very ill and you think about them profoundly in the hope that your memories become entangled with the garment itself. It's supposed to help you make peace with them before they, before they go."

"Well I've never heard of it, but you're a smart girl. The smartest in the building."

The men and the gurney had already gone up in the elevator, and when it returned she stepped into it alone and let Mr. Miller hit the button for the sixth floor. In that mirrored vessel moving upward she saw nothing but her father all around her—floating, standing upright, dressed in his suit, dressed in his death gown, trimming his mustache, taking his medicine. The journey seemed as if it was going on forever and she wondered if the sweater was the cause, the memory sweater, as she had now named it. When they put him in the ground in his giant coffin, would she still be able to conjure him using this garment?

Her mother was barely conscious, pale as snow on her bed as the men prepared the body for removal in the next room. Doctor Scholdt was hovering above her, holding a cigarette in one hand and squeezing her fingers with the other. A leather valise holding a set of hypodermic needles lay open on the bed.

"If you can feel me squeezing, then all's well, Mrs. Darder. You just breathe slow and let the men do their job. You'll be able to visit Mr. Darder at the funeral home tomorrow."

Was it possible that she had seen the black men touching her husband? Probably, so it was a good thing that she was sedated. When the doctor noticed Anna standing there his whole body tightened and turned like a screw.

"*You*," he said, "almost sent your mother to join your father."

"I'm here now. I want to see him."

"Then do so." Turning to his patient, he said, "Your daughter has arrived and is fine," and her mother made a sound of relief, but so deep in a haze was she that not a single word was comprehendible.

"Arrl, zahrlahary ich ovin."

One of the men preparing the body for removal had a flat nose, thick lips, and wide-set eyes, the kind of features her father had taught here were "niggeroid," and her father would have said that they probably made this man stupider than the other one, who was taller with a beautiful aquiline nose, a crew cut (as if he were in the army), and high cheekbones.

"Well hello little girl," the one with the flatter nose said. "He was quite a big boy, your father was, but we'll get him out of here without a single bruise or scrape, you'll see." He had his hands all over her father, removing his glasses and placing them in a box for effects, then smoothing back his hair in a motherly fashion, and with a few gentle strokes clearing his forelock from his forehead, putting his fingers through the spare, countable strands so that they were separated evenly and all slicked back uniformly. Seeing that configuration made her think about parallel lines, parallel lines of the non-Euclidean sort, about which her father had taught her. The man now bent down and looked into her father's eyes as he shut them with four fingers. The other, soldierly one said, "Hurry up Ben, let's not make a show of it."

"Just doing good by the dead," Ben said.

"Well let's get on with it and give this poor girl some peace and quiet."

"Pick out a good dark suit for him," Ben said to the other, who then began sorting through the hangers in the closet.

Then the white man, the leader of the two, came in. He was short and Anna figured that with his triangular features, hairy hands, and calculating eyes, he must be a Jew. He told Anna to leave the room "unless you wanna see your daddy naked," which she never had and didn't want to now.

Back in the bedroom, Dr. Scholdt was wrapping up his visit, packing his bag and leaving an envelope by her mother's nightstand. Anna felt like she could easily lay herself down right next to her mother and sleep for the rest of the year, just like that.

"She'll be disoriented when she first wakes up, so if you or the nurse could be here, it would be helpful."

"I'll stay," Anna said. "She'll be okay?"

"Sure thing. It's a big event, death of a spouse and so forth. And you didn't help, little girl."

"I'm fifteen. Not so little when you think about it. And my father's dead."

"True, that's certainly true, and I'm sorry for you," and he left the room, trailing a single whorl of cigarette smoke that grew bigger and bigger and then disappeared into the air. She held the sweater to her chest.

Standing on a chair, hands on the window, she had to cock her head and look steeply down in order to see the street and sidewalk below. She wanted to watch the men load her father into the hearse, an image she knew she'd hold onto forever. Her heart nearly broke through her chest when she saw, waiting opposite her building and looking up toward her, Arabelle. Only something was wrong, for she was at least twice the size as before, a gargantuan girl with the same relative proportions, the same dimpled chin and shiny thick hair, the same piercing, jewel-like eyes. When the undertakers finally emerged, a small crowd of passersby gathered to watch, but nobody seemed to notice the black girl who towered over them. It took some time to slide the large man and the gurney into the back of the hearse. The car visibly sank on its suspension. At last the men closed the double back doors and proceeded next to load themselves into the vehicle. But Arabelle opened those two back doors and bent double and, like a contortionist, ducked into the hearse with Anna's father, looking up toward Anna with a little devious smile before closing the doors from within. Then the powerful engine started with a rumble, and the hearse moved off toward Third Avenue.

Lessons

I'm hanging out in Washington Square Park on an exceptionally warm March afternoon. Everyone's out because it's almost sixty degrees and the taste of spring is too much to resist. There was a foot of snow a week earlier, and now it's all but gone. On a patch of soggy green between a few sycamore trees three college students—two girls and a guy—are tossing a Frisbee around. I'm a good Frisbee player, played on an ultimate team in high school and a little in college. "Hey," I say, "mind if I toss the disc with you guys?" I can tell by the way they look at me that they think I'm a square if not creepy older guy. I am older than them, in my thirties.

Hesitantly, they let me in and I get between the two girls.

I toss the disc with them for a while and they seem somewhat impressed with my skill and accuracy. Eventually we get to introducing ourselves—it's really at my prompting. "I'm Don," I shout to the girl at my left. "Mary," she shouts back, throwing me the Frisbee. "Earl," the guy says, "Janet," the other girl. It's like we're all about to break into song. Now we know each other and the tosses get freer and a little more daring.

Earl throws one too hard over Janet's head and it lands on the asphalt pretty far away. I run, leap over the little wrought iron fence, pick up the disc, and toss it from where I am back to her. It soars over a couple of bystanders' heads, banks left, slows just in time (the rim lifting in front) and Janet catches it. "Nice throw, Don!" she shouts, a lingering smile, white teeth.

We play for a while more and I try to teach Janet a forehand throw based on wrist motion. I decide I like her over Mary because she's got that smile, has a nice body, and will talk to me. She has trouble with the throw so I stand beside her—close, probably too—and demonstrate. "It's all in the wrist," I say. "Think of your arm as a whip and your hand as the end of the whip. So watch. I'm moving my arm back at the shoulder then as I get down to the end of my arm I stop short, like pulling the whip back, and *snap*. And this is when you let the Frisbee go . . . like this." And I throw a long smooth one to Earl.

"I think I'm getting it," Janet says a few minutes later, catching a throw from Mary, "but show me again." I stand behind her and lightly put her arm through the correct throwing motion ending with a light pull on her wrist to indicate the whip-like motion. She does it on her own and throws a decent toss across the battled green to Mary. "Getting there," I say to her.

Eventually Janet says that she and Mary and Earl have to get to class. "Can I call you sometime?" I ask. She seems a little taken aback so I say, "You've got the throw down pretty good, but a little more time with me and you'll have it down perfectly."

"I'll tell you what," she says, "why don't I meet you here tomorrow at the same time and you can teach me some more."

"That's fine," I say.

She smiles, thanks me, joins her two friends who are already crossing Washington Square South. When I'm about six blocks from the park I realize that I've taken their Frisbee, have been carrying it the whole time without even knowing it. I used to carry one of them around with me wherever I went and somehow that feeling is back, the nervous pathways or whatever are awake again.

Next day it's just Janet and me. It's about ten degrees colder than the day before and there are fewer people in the park. "Sorry about taking the disc. You probably thought I was a scam artist or petty thief of some kind."

"It crossed my mind," she says, "but you didn't seem the type."

"Sometimes I wouldn't mind seeming the type, wouldn't mind instilling a little fear in people."

"Why on earth would you want to?" she says.

"People respect that kind of power in this city," I say, adding, "You're invisible if you're too passive or passive-looking." I don't know why, but she laughs at me. I show her that throw again and she continues to get better at it, me at the other end of the clearing and she throwing it to me. We go on like that for about an hour until she says that it's time for her to go to class. "Is it too early for me to ask for your number again?" I say. "Because I was just thinking that maybe we could get lunch, or only coffee, or nothing at all next time, instead of throwing the Frisbee." She takes out a pen and paper and writes out her full first and last names and her number beneath them. "I'll call you soon but not too soon," I say. "That's good," she says, "because now I'm convinced you're not a creep just scoping out the park for co-eds." I laugh it off as though it were the most ludicrous suggestion in the world.

I call her the same night because I've got a serious question. "Listen," I say, "I know this might seem strange, but you have a very unusual last name, the same last name as a well known author who happens to be one of my favorites. And now, as I'm saying this, I'm also looking at a picture of him from when he was younger on the dust jacket of one of his novels—*Prim Lies*—and I'm realizing that the resemblance is remarkable." Silence for a few seconds. "Well now you're onto me," she says. She sounds let down—now her big secret's out. "I'm his daughter but wish I weren't. The fact is I don't like the kind of notoriety I get, as if I've *inspired* him."

"But, but," I stammer, "His daughters, or *daughters* in general, are such an important part of his writing. His most famous novel—oh God, I'm on the spot and its name escapes me. It's about a writer and, you got it, his daughter. And...I know I don't have to tell you—but it's such a tightly woven, seemingly personal narrative that I can't imagine it's not autobiographical."

"You're talking about the one that takes place in the Florida Keys," Janet says, "where they visit Hemingway's bungalow."

"Yes!" I say, "*Key West*. That's its name. Where he carries the older daughter into the ocean. What an incredible scene! How he wades in with her and explains the breaking waves—how they're the pulse of the ocean—and that she's not to be frightened because he's holding her so ardently and would never let anything bad happen to her. He actually uses the word 'ardently' to the little girl, as if she'll know what it means. But I suppose the daughter of a writer gets started early. Anyway, when she does get scared he stops and turns, pointing to her mother and younger sister back on the beach and has her wave to them. 'Look,' he says. 'Land ho!'"

"Lies," Janet says, simply enough.

"But the details," I say, "how he's decided that since this is his daughter's first time going into ocean water he's got to make it a warm and memorable experience. How he holds her up as waves break around them, the spray and foam splashing over them both. His daughter laughs, claps her hands in excitement. He finally goes back to shore and her mother, his wife, dries her off—"

"Yes yes," Janet says, "I *know* the story. And I've explained this to other people: we did visit Hemingway's bungalow and my father did bring us to the beach but he ignored us as he got plastered on margaritas. My mother didn't come because she'd had enough of him.

"He was drunker than hell and dragged me into the water and threw me into a wave while my sister watched. She started to scream. She thought I would drown. The wave threw me hard into broken shells or whatever, and I got a gash in my shoulder. A few years ago I might've shown you the scar and believe me, you'd be impressed. It's got Dad's signature all over it. He pulled me out by the wrists, still laughing, like the whole thing would be forgotten in a couple of minutes, and if not, I'd be all the stronger for it. I still remember him saying something like 'Don't fret my dear, you'll thank me for this later.'"

It's unbelievable, I think. In the photos I've seen of her father his eyes are full of warmth and omniscience, and he's reported to have quite a depth of character. I've seen him read at New

York cafés and bookstores and he always seems patient and respectful and even flattered that he still gets so much attention. "The wick refuses to go out," he's been known to say.

"My father was a terror to be around," Janet says. "I ran away twice by the time I was seventeen. Always got scared and came back in the end, but that should tell you something, Don. What does it tell you—the fact that I left in the first place?"

"I get your drift," I say. "There's plenty of misery to go around in this world."

"He'd have other women in the house if Mom went away for even a couple of days. They'd make sounds—laughter, drunk laughter and these sex noises—with me and my sister in the next room. It was a real comedy. The guy's a goddamn nightmare is what he is. Yeah, he's a brilliant writer, I'll give him that."

"Very brilliant," I burst out.

"Okay," she says, "we'll say very brilliant. Would love to have inherited that gene, but I bet it's hitched to the cruel, misogynistic trait as well, and I'd want no part of that, or whatever the female equivalent is. It's mathematics for me all the way. It's precise, has a high utility, and gets me out of competition with him."

"I understand," I say. "I'm sorry you feel this way—or sorry that you've been put through what you have. Maybe I can call you again in a few days? We can just forget about this conversation altogether. Just press the *clear cache* button. However you people put that."

"Don, don't worry about bringing up these memories. I've got to go over this every time some literature buff discovers who I am. But please don't call again. I'm really hoping to meet somebody who's got a knack for numbers and has never read a word my father's written," and she hangs up.

Garage Door

While passing through my childhood neighborhood on the way back from a job interview, I stop at the house I grew up in and tell the owners I want to buy their garage door. A man slams the front door in my face, but I knock again and he opens it. His tie hangs loosened around his open-collared white shirt. He's probably taken the train up from the city and sat down for dinner a few minutes ago, just a regular business guy with a start-up family who has to break his ass to make it all work. His two kids and wife are watching me from behind him. Probably she works all day as well. I want to tell them I'm not dangerous, that I know every corner of their house, that my childhood lurks in every crevice, though that probably wouldn't be a good idea.

"Please listen to me," I say. "When I was six it was 1971 and my mother and I painted flowers, peace signs, and the words 'Love and Peace' on that garage door. It was late summer, August probably. I remember it clearly; it's one of my most vivid memories in fact. When I was ten it was 1975 and my parents put this house on the market. The first thing they did was paint over the flowers and the peace sign and the words."

"It's a strange request, mister, and we're eating dinner now," he says.

"Strange request? I'll give you that."

Then I remember how my mother outfitted me with a little painter's cap that she had folded and tied out of a rag. And my father was also out back digging a drainage ditch at the low point of the yard to prevent it from flooding whenever it rained hard. He was shirtless, skinny and tall, sweating, and his black body hair stuck to his skin like paintbrush bristles.

"Come back tomorrow," this young father says, "and we'll see what we can do. But I'm not making any promises." And he closes the door again.

I take a look down the driveway and there it is, same garage, presumably with the same garage door. They've put a hoop up over it so that their kids and the kids in the neighborhood can play basketball. That's good, I think. We should have done that, but weren't big on athletics or kids bouncing basketballs all day in our driveway. I wonder how many layers of paint are insulating the flowers, peace sign and words from the abuse of these kids. The door's yellow or off-white—it's getting dark out so I can't quite tell—with scuff marks all over it. What I failed to tell the owners of sixty-six Quinby Avenue is that I now live an hour-and-a-half drive away.

Even so, I return the next day at around noon, with my pickup. I knock on the front door and ring the bell of the house I grew up in, but there's no answer. I wait, knock again, ring again, and still there's no answer. I walk around back and peer in through a set of new bay windows that weren't there when we lived in the house, but the place is empty and dark inside. Behind one of the closed windows a fat calico cat is stretched out on the sill in the summer light. When it sees me it rolls over and arches to expose its soft underside. A cat, that's also something we didn't have.

I back my truck down the driveway, take out my toolkit and ladder, and get to work. As far as garage doors go, it's a smaller, wooden one, but takes a while to remove anyway. It's got a number of rusty steel struts, cables and, most dangerous of all, the extension springs that helps the door open and close. Nonetheless, I manage to get the thing off its track without major injury. Because the door's articulated, I fold it into fourths and slide it into the back of the pickup. On a piece of my stationery I write them a note thanking them for the door, and slip one hundred dollars in cash with it into an envelope. This is money I don't have, cash I took out of an ATM as an advance on my Visa. I put the envelope in their mail slot and start the drive home.

When I get there my son, Alex, is out back getting ready to launch an Estes model rocket. "You won't be able to get that back if you launch it from here," I tell him. "Wait until Saturday and I'll take you out to Robin's Field. You need lots of space."

He ignores me for about a minute during which time I stand there waiting for his acknowledgment like a clerk awaiting his next task. "I'm experimenting," he finally says. "I'm gonna find an ant and stick it in the nosecone. It's like when they launched the dog into orbit. We just learned about it. Were you born yet?"

"I don't know. I don't think so. Anyway, they let the dog die," I tell him. "The Ruskies. They never planned on getting it back." Alex stops his myopic hunt for an ant and looks at me.

"Die? It never came back?" He stares at the ground blankly. "My ant's gonna come back though," he says, turning over a small stone and raking the dirt beneath it with a stick. I head inside.

My wife, Nadine, is in the kitchen frying up chicken livers and onions, which—along with boxed macaroni and cheese—has become our staple. I've been out of work for about six months now and the money's all but gone. Luckily, Nadine makes a little off-the-books cash cleaning houses during the day and I'm about ready to join her.

"Rice?" I say to her.

"On the stove." I lift the top off the pot and there's the clumpy Minute Rice, the scourge of my life.

"Tomorrow night I'll make some good old fashioned rice," I say, "instead of this freeze dried crap."

"Same story I get every night," she says.

"I will, I swear it." Alex comes in and I tell him to wash his hands. I set the table as my wife finishes the cooking.

I married too young. That much I'm sure of. Nadine is still beautiful, still young. She was my first love, my only love, is the only woman with whom I've made love. A sprinter in high school, she's managed, seemingly without effort, to keep her athletic looks. Meaning she's slim and tenacious, wiry and strong. But lately I've noticed some new lines, worry lines, around her eyes.

I'm their cause. One of those inexplicable laws of marriage says that spouses can grow distant, that they can lose sight of the qualities that first drew them together in perceived inseparability. First loves have a certain pungency as well, a juvenile association with the discovery of sex and intimacy and shared lives that's bound to grow old fast. Our son, product of one of many lusty nights Nadine and I spent with each other during winter break from our respective colleges, is the one who will pay the price when we split. Alex will be the loser, that we both know, and yet neither of us has addressed it directly.

We sit down at the table and eat in silence. Alex is thinking about the dog in space, starving, suffocating, or freezing, Mission Control—or whatever the Soviets called it—observing the blips of its last heartbeats. Just a dog, just an ant. I shouldn't have said what I did about it. Poor kid. I was about his age when my mother and I painted the garage door.

After dinner I stand in the kitchen alone and wash the dishes. I hear a muffled British voice coming from the television in the living room and know that Nadine and Alex are watching "Nature," and David Attenborough is probably narrating the mating rituals of Peruvian butterflies, or something like that. I stare out the open window above the sink. It faces our backyard and blackness. The night is steamy and though the window's been open, the kitchen is unbearably hot and the air is still; not even the slightest current comes in through the screen. Over the sound of the television the crickets sing. A mosquito's been buzzing me all along, a hypodermic needle with wings, as I imagine it, that's found its way to me.

When I'm done with the dishes, I sneak out, carrying my work gloves, wearing a thick thrift shop work shirt that has "Ambrose" embroidered on the pocket. Outside, by the shed, I set up.

Knee-high in thistle, I work illuminated by a lamp on an extension cord and the dim light coming from the house. The interstate hums a half-mile away. In the thick summer air its sound carries well. I brush a light coat of diluted paint stripper on the garage door, which I've propped up on the outside of the tool shed. Diluted because I don't want to rush things and remove that evidence of my childhood. Nonetheless, it's strong stuff. A spider living in the joints between the garage door segments falls victim to the fumes. It withers, its legs interlocking like spiked teeth around its aspirin-sized body, then is still, except that it rotates one way then the other on a single strand of web, its last bit of life transformed into kinetic motion. A moth or two circle the lamp on the ground a few feet away. The fumes form an insecticidal shroud around me. Nothing comes close, but I hear the tiny buzzings and the flutter of rice paper wings in the dark all around me.

I work carefully, slowly, with a small scraper and a soft steel brush. After a half-hour the first layer of paint, a kind of piss yellow, begins to blister and fall away. There's another layer, of gray, beneath that, and it too falls away with some work. Beneath it is white and I can see beneath that some faded figures and letters, bright colors trying to break through. I go even lighter on the paint thinner and switch to steel wool.

I've now been outside in the dark for several hours and nobody seems to care that I haven't returned to the house. The television's still on, I can see, throwing its muted multicolor flashes against the living room ceiling. Probably Alex staying up late, which I shouldn't permit. I suppose Nadine can see me from the bedroom window and she considers that I'm involved in yet another innocuous project that has nothing to do with getting us out of debt or nullifying the marriage, or at least trying to satisfy our sexual needs. Very carefully I remove the layer of paint that obscures the flowers and peace sign and words. It comes off slowly but beautifully, melting away in dime-sized flecks, revealing the bright fuchsias and yellows, the innocent, youthful blue, the peace sign in black. It's all there, exactly as I remember it. Mom was my age, I was Alex's. I step into the darkness, away from the work lamp, out of the fumes, because I want to see how this remnant of my childhood looks framed by the night. It is displaced, ludicrously propped up in the tattered present.

A mosquito buzzes past my ear. No doubt it will drill into me and extract some blood for its sustenance. In this, I believe, I am a good find.

Next morning, no surprise, there's a cop car in the driveway. Stolen property. Mrs. Ravieli is out in her garden, wearing her slippers and Oshkosh overalls, watching the sergeant deal with me in that civil, country way people seem to believe has gone out of fashion. Sergeant Smith is his name, the rare African American policeman in white Ponderosa Station.

"The gentlemen this belongs to called the police station and explained the note you left him. He said he'll consider it a loan, doesn't want to file any charges."

"I'll bring it back today."

"The sooner the better. And what the hell is this all about, anyway, Chuck?"

"Look at it," I say. "I was my kid's age when I helped my mom paint that."

"Very impressive. Return it now."

He gets into his Ford cruiser and backs out of the driveway, neighbors' heads turning as he drives at 7 M.P.H. away from the house, down Bramble Hill Lane. Saturday morning, blue skies, and the whole block is out tending their yards and cultivating gossip. I'm standing out there with a hell of a mosquito bite on my neck. Experiment over.

I put the door back into the pickup along with a gallon of primer. If they want me to paint over everything, I'll do it when I get there.

When I do get there, the father's playing catch with one of his sons out in the front yard. He's a bigger guy than he looked at the front door. Bigger than me and I'm guessing he works out, and is a football coach sort of guy. All strategy and metaphor. Clean shaven, fresh buzz cut. He starts walking toward the truck before I even stop. I roll down the window.

"Well well," he says, "our mental patient has returned with our property." I hadn't noticed it, but one of his ears is severely clipped, like you'd see on some purebred dogs.

"Thanks for not pressing charges. I guess it would have been a pain in the ass for both of us."

"Watch the language." He looks back at his kid, who's standing in the driveway spinning the football. He hands me back my envelope. "I kept twenty dollars as a service fee. You know what you're doing, putting that thing back on its tracks, or do you need my help?"

"I'll let you know. Mind if I back down the driveway?"

"You didn't ask the first time, why now," and he motions for his kid to move out of the way.

When I get down to the garage I see his wife—a slim woman with magenta streaks dyed into her brown hair—looking out at me through those bay windows. She's shaking her head, and then it looks like she enters something into her PDA. The house has lost its charge for me now and I suddenly see the situation as every other person in the world would see it, and I'm pretty embarrassed. I just want to get out of there. Unlike stealing a garage door, reinstalling it is really not a one man job. It needs to be set into the track on both sides at once, something that I'm not capable of doing on my own. I decide this after twenty minutes of trying and providing a show, no doubt.

Finally, the football coach comes down. "I'm going to help you now," he says. His breath is minty, as if his wife said he should brush his teeth before speaking to the insane. You never know exactly what might set them off.

"That's kind of you," I say.

"It would be better for everyone if you were to leave sooner rather than later."

I see that the daughter, who's maybe twelve, has brought some of her friends around and they're at the top of the driveway now, watching us, two grown men on our knees looking at this artifact.

We get the door reinstalled and there are no big surprises. The hardest part is getting the extension springs in place without taking off a finger. The door still works fine. I get some oil from my toolkit and lube the tracks and springs.

"You know it's not so bad," the father says, looking at the flowers and all. "I mean there's nothing like this going on these days. If my kids wanted to do something like this we wouldn't even consider it."

"Then you think you might leave this the way it is?"

"Are you kidding?"

I pack up my tools and get ready to leave. His wife observes again from the bay window and I wave to her, just to watch her respond, which she does with a little demi-wave down about hip level, PDA still in hand.

I honk twice as I pull back onto the street, as if these are my friends and I'll be seeing them again soon.

Grey

It's the tail end of the twentieth century, an autumn afternoon, and in the darkened corner of an East Village tenement apartment, Grey DeSilva slouches on an ancient sofa. His windows are barred with security gates and covered in grit and nicotine and he is surrounded by pile upon pile of detritus, from newspapers and art books to eviscerated transistor radios. Punctuating this landscape are teetering stacks of white polyhedral Chinese take-out containers.

On the television an advertisement shows young men and women frolicking in the surf, laughing as they languidly throw their unworked bodies at one another. The young men, impossibly slim, are devoid of any body hair while the women's firm bodies shimmer with beads of sea water. Grey follows the action exactingly, as if fighting to comprehend this curious, libidinous circus. "Have fun," a woman's voice, mature and sultry, says, her tone intimating that these young and fresh Americans will be screwing each other until the sun comes up, "but be safe." The advertisement is for a popular brand of condoms and so brief that he questions whether he misheard something.

A twenty-year-old wall calendar is stuck on June, as if this were the year and month of his own death. His phone rings only when a credit agency or utility company reminds him of unpaid bills, of pending legal action or a utility shut-off. He then pays his bills immediately, although the envelopes usually come back the first time around because of insufficient postage. Like his calendar, his stamps are also out of date. Framed photos once hung on these walls but over the course of a couple of decades he's taken them down one by one during drunken, lachrymose fits of nostalgia, as if the objects in the photos—his brother, an ex-girlfriend, the Sandia Mountains of New Mexico, where he'd once gone hiking with friends—had somehow betrayed him. Some of the photos still exist, frameless, buried, pocked from shards of glass. They have migrated halfway across the apartment not unlike a vein of granite affected by tectonic uplift.

As the afternoon extends into early evening, the sun shines into the apartment but casts no definable shadows. The condom ad still reeling in his mind, Grey listens to the bleating of rush hour traffic on the streets below. He tries to deduce from the frequency and severity of horn honks the mood of the city. But tonight there is another racket, this one coming from the stairwell. His upstairs neighbor, Genevieve "Genie" Tettenbaum is finally moving out. Her kids, he has gleaned from the snippets of conversation that drift into his apartment, are putting her in a Baltimore nursing home, close to where one of them lives. She has become arthritic, absent-minded, frail.

He lights a Phillies Blunt and drops the extinguished match onto the floor. So many years' worth of them make a sort of topsoil, a soft insulating layer in which other, smaller, residents of the city also live.

Although new images are now on the television, he sees only the young men and women in the condom ad. In his mind he has stripped off their insignificant bikinis and swimming briefs, conjured their breasts and asses, the narrow hips of the men, the women's sexes. It has been so long since he's seen one at close range that his shame rises when he cannot picture the major and minor attributes. He tries to recall when that time was. After a minute or so he concludes it was around 1979 and her name was Jeanette Falco, a local locksmith who can still be seen around the neighborhood, now with her teenage daughter in tow as an apprentice. Jeanette came to his rescue one drunken night when he'd lost his keys while at a bar on First Avenue. After she'd drilled out the old lock cylinder they went inside and he opened a bottle of Rhone wine and convinced her to take a load off, smoke a joint with him, hang out and listen to some John Coltrane. He was still passably handsome then—tall, lean, completely uninhibited—and always drunk for one reason or another. His chest hair had started turning silver in patches. He remembers pulling her jeans off—they were covered in graphite dust and glided off her body silently—and shaking his head with pleasure when he discovered that she wasn't wearing anything under them. Afterward, she took out her work order pad, scrawled a bill and handed it to him. It was for seventy-five dollars. Her taste was still in his mouth as he wrote her a check. She tapped in the new lock cylinder, handed him the keys, and left.

As much he wants to stay focused on his old bones and fading libido, he cannot easily distract himself from the goings on in the stairwell. Genie Tettenbaum, his neighbor and sometimes friend for thirty years, a woman a generation older than him, is being taken lightly by the hand and marched off to the final chapter of her life.

She and her husband, Hugh, moved into the building in 1967, only a year after Grey. While race riots were burning other cities—Newark, New Haven, Detroit—New York was smoldering, smoking, but somehow never fully catching fire. At the time of the Tettenbaum's arrival, Grey was starting his Masters' Degree in mechanical engineering at City College, more to stay out of Vietnam than advance himself within the Establishment. Hugh and Genie had already been married for fifteen years and had decided to cash in their suburban life in Westchester and live a grand experiment. With their adolescent son and daughter at their side, they packed their belongings into the sixth floor apartment above Grey's. Something about their close quarters, the dangers of the city, the lingering odor a century of immigrant life brought to the neighborhood drew in the Tettenbaums, seduced them where it repelled most others. Grey understands this essence that lingered in the air, an essence all gone now, wiped clean but for the buildings themselves, tenements whose fire escapes were once festooned with hand wrung garments drying in the sun instead of chrysanthemums, cat grass and bonsai gardens. Hugh and Genie's grand experiment ended in 1993 when Hugh died of a heart attack.

A dresser bangs against his door on its way down the steps and his reverie is interrupted. An adolescent girl is whining in the hallway. "I want Ben and Jerry's. You *said* we can get Ben and Jerry's if we helped." A strained voice, her father's: "Soon." When Grey hears the people move off he peeks his head out the door and sees dust bunnies, flakes of old newspaper, dried bits of potpourri trailing past his door and down the steps. These weightless objects, he thinks, these incidental scraps of Genie's past, this is the dust of a life that has already ended. The thought of having an old geezer roommate, of living in a building that smells like piss, where your meals arrive on plastic trays, these things scare the sex right out of him. For a moment, looking around the squalid apartment, he notes the absurdity of his surroundings, the impossibility of having arrived here. It is as if somebody is playing a joke on him.

When he first met her, Genie used to climb the stairs quickly and silently, carrying bags of groceries and wine, a child sometimes following behind her, huffing, complaining, trying to keep up. He would spy her through his peephole. She was tall, awkward on her little feet, and quite beautiful, with high cheekbones, sandy brown hair going gray, narrow hips and dark blue eyes. He didn't know what her maiden name was, but he always suspected that it was something single-syllabic and Waspy—Dent, Webb, Pierce.

Now, in old age, her height worked against her, added a tenuousness to the way she moved. The last time Grey saw her was one afternoon about a month ago. He was coming back from a cigar and booze run and she was out on the stoop, plumbing her old purse for her lobby key, which she constantly misplaced. He held the lobby door open for her and led her inside.

"I need help with a stuck window," she said suddenly. "Can you come up tonight?"

"Wish I could, Genie, but I pulled a muscle down *there* the other day. Sore as hell. Doc says take it easy with the lifting."

And he smiled at her as if everything he said was valid and truthful and all was well. From past experience he knew the real reason for her beckoning to him: she would pull out old photos of Hugh, then review the lives of her children, the vital stats of the three grandchildren and then, invariably, she would begin to weep for her lost soulmate and the cruelties the passage of time has visited upon her body. And so he rarely went to see her, preferring instead the occasional coincidence of meeting on the stairwell or stoop.

Outside, street lamps are beginning to go on. Genie's children and grandchildren carry the last of her belongings past Grey's door, down the steep steps, and load them into what he imagines to be a big U-Haul parked out front. He realizes that he now occupies the last rent-controlled apartment in the building. Next time it will be he whose life is being boxed up and loaded onto a truck. But by whom he cannot imagine. He has no children, no wife, only alienated distant cousins strewn around the globe.

It also dawns on him, suddenly, that she is going to say goodbye to him, that Genie would not leave without saying goodbye. He brushes his hair and teeth, finds some reasonably clean clothing and dons a pair of black loafers he finds under the kitchen sink in a plastic bag. Remarkably, they have held their shine over the decades since he last wore them. He keeps his ear to the door until he hears the slow ticking of her cane on the slate as she climbs the stairs. She knocks on his door. He opens it and there she stands, alone, somehow shorter than he expected, diminished. He can see some blue veins under the skin of her forehead. But her eyes are deep and blue and as clear as he'd ever seen them. "At least I won't have to climb these damn stairs anymore," she says. She presses something into Grey's palm. "If Hugh were here he would insist you take this." It is a fold of bills.

"No," he says, stunned, a bolt of heat and anger suddenly rising up in him. "I've got some savings. I'm fine."

"Buy yourself some clothing, food, whatever it is you need most. Just no liquor. You see what's happened, don't you? You're stuck fast."

"Genie," he says, placing the bills back into her hand and firmly closing her small, dry fist around them, "I'm going to fix myself up, I promise." He does not believe his own words, but hearing them said aloud makes such an undertaking seem almost feasible. "Now get out of here," he says.

"At least escort me down the stairs."

"I'd be no good. I'm drunk." This, at least, is the truth.

Then they embrace a little stiffly and he watches her go.

Ten minutes later he hears the rental truck start and tracks the diesel engine's idle as it pulls into cross-town traffic. It is a quiet, calm evening, with only a few distant horn honks. He closes his eyes and listens for as long as he can to the truck as it moves away. He wonders if her things will be unpacked for her or if they will be put in storage, only to be tallied for the reckoning of her estate. He manages to track the truck's engine for almost a minute, but soon it blends into the sound of the city, a constant, never-ending droning, the sound of life moving forward.

Another New York Love Story

It was me and Alexandra, and Marvin and his girlfriend at the time, I remember her name was Sally, and a handful of other friends and acquaintances who I'd known for a while. We were out for dinner and drinks at a bar-restaurant in Alphabet City, and it was late. Marvin was getting upset about something, which he did fairly often. His being upset wasn't anything that would get your heart rate up but I could see how Sally might get annoyed. And she started saying, to calm him down, "It's okay, Boo. We'll go to another place, Boo, and get dessert there."

And he said, "Honey, I like it when you call me Boo. That's sweet. But I like it more when you don't talk."

"And when's that?" I said, which I shouldn't have done.

"There are two times," Marvin said, as if he'd rehearsed the answer. "When she's sleeping and when my dick is in her mouth."

"Now that's too goddamned much," Margie said, laughing from the other end of the table.

We were very drunk at this place on East 7th Street. Way east. Ten years ago it was dangerous to be white and down around here, now it's swamped with suburban kids in truckers' hats and jeans they wear below their hips, the fashion that we've all heard so much whining about. The Dominicans and Puerto Ricans and blacks got pushed farther and farther east, into the river.

"A year-and-a-half," Sally said, putting her arm around Marvin, "and he still can't find my button. It's like an Easter egg hunt every night. 'Where'd she hide it now?' Ever read 'The Purloined Letter,' my dear? It's right in front of your face."

"The thrill of the hunt," he said. "And it has something to do with *you*, you know. You're a bit shy down there. Or maybe, oh Christ, or maybe I just don't do it for you."

It was my round, so I went up and got us pints of beer, glasses of wine, shots of tequila. When I came back another couple was talking.

"What a cutie he was when we first met," Shayla was saying, looking at her fingernails then turning to her boyfriend, Michael. "You remember that SMS you sent to me at the cafe?"

Michael, who looked something like a third century Dane, replete with a little dirt around his eyes and a red, patchy beard that might have been hiding a scar, was sitting next to her. He remained silent.

"First you sent a message that said 'go to the ladies' room,'" she said. "Then you sent one that said 'set your phone on vibrate and hold it to your clit.' Well I did as I was told like a good little girl, and you just kept sending SMSs." They were holding hands now as if they were talking about some great expedition where he'd repelled a grizzly. "Didn't matter what they said, right? One letter. One letter. One letter. Oh god. You actually made me come like that. From like what, a hundred miles away?"

"I was between meetings in Philly," he said.

"Well you never did that again."

"You never asked." He picked up a glass of wine and held it out in a sort of tenuous half toast to himself. I don't think he knew he was doing it.

"Why would I have to ask?" she said.

"You just did," he said, leaning over and kissing her on the forehead. "Tell them about your movie idea," he said.

"It's not really a movie, per se. More of a performance art piece called *Movie*. It goes like this: we set up to shoot a film down on Avenue A. You know, generator trucks, light cranes, reflectors, good-looking kids with ear-pieces and clipboards. We'd get a legitimate shooting permit, cone off all the parking spots. Generally piss off half the people on the block. But the truth is there is no cast, no script, nothing. Well, that's a little off. The cast consists of all these acting students pretending they're gaffers, assistant directors, and location people, whatever. As onlookers poke their heads in and ask what's going on, we would tell them it's a De Niro film called *Alphabet*."

"And then?" someone said.

"And then? Well, we see what happens. We could make a documentary about the non-film or we could create buzz about the non-film until the press picked it up and it was all exposed. I don't know, I think it's brilliant."

"So do I," said Michael. "I'm trying to get some investors together."

"That's 'cause you're my daddy," Shayla said to him.

"And you're my little bitch."

As I remember it, Alexandra was quiet during most of this, holding my hand under the table. She'd only met this group of friends once when we'd started dating, and that was down at the East River Park. We'd been tossing a Frisbee around in the month of June, a bunch of late-thirties and early-forties geeks-with-paunches whose bodies were just beginning to fail. The point being, at that gathering we had all been sober and our mouths were pretty clean. But when we all got a buzz on, things went downhill pretty quickly. This was the way things went with the gang. Assholes, pussies, clits, prostates, testes, cum, cocks, mouths, tits, cervixes, uteruses, babies—these and not much else were the topics up for discussion.

"So . . ." Margie said, looking at Alexandra, who I thought was the beauty at the table, or at least the freshest looking thing going, the newest sacrificial virgin. At thirty-four this wasn't exactly the case, but some of these friends of mine looked like they'd lived their lives on a non-stop merry-go-round. "So," Margie said, "You and Curtis."

"Curtis and I," Alexandra said back to her.

"How long have you two had your thing going on now?" Margie said.

"Six months, I think," she said, turning to me. "Your Curtis here is a sweet man." "Sweet as honey," Margie said. "But have you found, Alexandra, that he's a bit of a pushover?"

"Yes and no," Alexandra said, leaning into me, her long dark hair brushing against my face. She squeezed my hand under the table again.

Yes, I squeezed back, here we go.

We were still fine-tuning the dynamics of our relationship then, but she was more of a sadist emotionally but a masochist sexually. In bed she liked being spanked, which helped her come like Jesus. And she liked it when I humiliated her verbally when we were doing it, and I could pretty much throw her around any which way I pleased as long as I stayed away from hitting the face, and no heavy bruising allowed. I'd spit in her hair and slick it back from her eyes when we were screwing. But when we weren't in bed she was the dominant, sporadically cruel one, rarely saying a kind word about me to me, acting as if our phone conversations were more chore than anything else. You could call this duality compensatory, complementary, the ying and the yang. However you wanted to define it, it was a consumer of psychic energy, not a generator of one. I lost ten pounds in the first two months of going out with her but came more often than I ever had. Several times I had to call in sick to my job because I was too tired to get out of bed. My work—at a commercial real estate office—began to suffer.

I'd had my share of high-drama relationships, but this one was something new. She'd walk around with bruises on her ass and I'd walk around with a bruised ego. Now you could say that a woman walking around with a bruised ass is in worse shape than a man walking around with a bruised ego, and in some ways you'd be right. Or at least if it were brought to a jury you can bet they'd rule for the bruised ass. But as a man walking around with a bruised ego, I often imagined how much easier it would be to have a bruised ass instead. Those bruises are short-lived and superficial, and though evidence of physical abuse, they are applied with a certain species of love. With ego bruises you walk around full of self-doubt and -loathing, feelings of inadequacy and vulnerability, wondering how you permit yourself to put up with such belittling injustices. You ask yourself how you have suddenly become a masochist. Because you receive so little reassurance, you begin to get paranoid, certain that your lover is about to walk out on you. There goes your baseline sanity, your ability to remain objective. You keep thinking, "she's gonna walk any day now." Alexandra kept me on my toes and she kept me constantly pissed off so that when it was time to screw I'd have the wherewithal to act toward her in precisely the manner she wished.

The answer to the question, why put up with it? is that you get to smack around a really fine ass a few times a week, the kind of fantasy I'll bet most men harbor but few will admit to. And when you're done smacking it around, and the two of you are lying in bed, and maybe she's smoking and you're sipping on a beer, all is serene, more so than a mountain pond on a breezeless morning. The two of you have pulled something miraculous off, a plummet into the dark reaches of human culpability and a re-emergence into the dull light of the bedroom. You become armed with the certain knowledge that you are alive. We'd tingle there next to each other, silent.

The point I'm trying to make in total is that back then Alexandra and I were interlocked in a not necessarily healthy manner but we *were* interlocked, and tightly so, nonetheless. And there we sat at a long table at a loud bar in Alphabet City and the conversation was beginning to take off and was heading in a direction that, as I've said, tended toward the bleak and the pornographic. And so on the conversation went, and we spilled our drinks and we made more and more trips to the rustic bathroom, and we teased each other and some of us threatened to defecate on the table and finally, at four, the bar closed and off we went into the gray morning, I leaning on Alexandra, filled with a combination of camaraderie, self-loathing, and a deep understanding that this grand city that had now sucked down almost two decades of my life had left behind, in payment, only nights like this and nights like this and nights like this. Yet, almost unbelievably, beside me was a woman on whom I could lean and on whom I did lean without hesitation. Where had she come from? I must never let her go.

I remember the stumbling epiphany as if it had taken place last night and I was dead sober, the way the air was spotted, how Alexandra leaned me up against a lamppost, looked me in the eye, right into the back of my head and said "I'm going to find us a taxi" so sweetly that I knew, without doubt, that this represented a kind of end for me, that no more could I meet at the long table and let history repeat and repeat and layer upon itself until the next time I felt this way—stumbling home by lamplight, epiphanies exploding overhead like palm-sized fireworks—I would be sixty, not forty, and I would say life's been decent now show me the door.

How strange, I remember thinking: I've learned to hate this woman on cue, to smack her around elegantly as if she were a side of Kobe beef—because that's what she wants from me at those moments. But I could not, for my life, hook into those feelings as I leaned against the lamppost. She was walking west toward Avenue C in hopes of finding a yellow cab and she wasn't so sober herself. Where were those impulses she'd trained me to conjure? What would we do when we got back to my place? I wanted to have sex but I knew my body was too wasted, was soggy to the core. It would be no use. So I started a familiar cycle in my mind. I looked at her hard as she walked away, pulled her clothing off with my eyes, envisioned what I'd do to her. What happened then? Well, nothing then. Nothing. I just wanted her to get the cab, and I wanted to feel her lean into me as we sped north to my apartment.

Something changed between us in the many months that followed that night. When we made love we really made love—it was all about love. Love love love. Neither of us brought up the change of behavior, the dropping off of the violence and sadomasochistic tendencies. Maybe, I thought, it had been an initiation for both of us, a test of dominance and submission, a gauge of who would be on top and when—a contest without a sure winner. After a year went by it was clearly a part of our past. I didn't bring it up but sometimes I missed the way we were when we first met, if only because I had never had that experience before, the being abused, the abusing, the sound of my palm on her flesh filling the bedroom chamber.

In my most vivid memory of that time, Alexandra tells me of a particular type of torture she wants me to inflict on her. I hear her out and then go into her kitchen and in a few minutes come back into the bedroom with a wooden spoon and a glass bowl filled with ice water. "Well hi there," she says when I come back in, the ice in the bowl clanking around, the wooden spoon bobbing up and down in the water like a fucked-up boat. I put the bowl of ice water beside the bed and wait for the spoon to get saturated and cold, and then I use the back of it on her. It goes on for half the night and when she finally climaxes she makes so much noise and commotion that neighbors in the adjacent apartments start pounding on the walls, adding to the sense that the universe is coming apart at the seams.

Where was this woman now? Where had she gone? Was that night just a dream, half nightmare, half sexual fantasy? I searched my mind but couldn't find the point in time when the behavior had discretely stopped or whether we'd ever had a discussion beforehand. Were the early months just a fiction I'd made up? I decided I'd open that door again, just a crack, enough to prove to myself that Alexandra and I had once been an entirely different couple.

So about a month ago, as we were having sex at my place, I started spanking her. Gently, playfully, a little tap-tap on her rump.

"Have you been a bad girl, you bitch?"

"No. I've been good. What do you mean, *bitch*?"

Then I spanked her a little harder and she pushed me out.

"What's up, babe?" she said.

"Bring back any memories?"

"Is that something you miss?"

"I was going to ask you the same question."

"I asked first," she said.

I got comfortable on my back and maintained myself. She lit up a cigarette.

"Sometimes," I said. "You know we can always try anything you want."

"You're so accommodating."

"Your turn," I said. "You miss it?"

"The physical stuff? Not particularly. It was a phase. But we can do it if you want to. It seems like it turns you on tonight. Just be gentle."

"Wasn't I always?"

"You were as gentle as a gorilla."

"And when did the patient cease in her desire to be batted around?" I said.

"*Batted around*. Is that the way think about it?"

"Basically, yes. How do you think about it?"

"Being humiliated, subjugated, infantilized, objectified," she said.

"A list. You've obviously thought about it."

"I lived it for a long time, longer than you want to know. It was what I needed to feel secure."

"You must still want it," I said.

"Why do you say that?"

"You just must. Why would things change so quickly for you?"

"Ever think it was you?" she said.

"It's possible. But to shed all of that . . . stuff just because of me. It's a daunting idea."

"You don't think highly enough of yourself."

"Or I don't believe you."

"Don't say that. And stop jerking off."

"I want to spank your ass," I said. "Stop your talking and bend over, woman."

"Look," she said, letting out twin jets of smoke, "you were too rough with me."

"I was?"

"It's my fault—I don't think you got it right the first time and I never corrected you. But I thought we moved on. I mean we *have* moved on, but it's obviously come back."

"How was I too rough?"

"You didn't understand how to hold your hand when you hit me. You should *cup* your hands, not hit flat. I liked it at first. Sort of cute and naive and it was a new type of pain. But after a while I began to worry about you. The whole thing was taking a toll on us, and you were changing."

"That's because you were always pissing me off. You wanted me to be angry all the time. You wanted me to be some mean-ass pipe fitter coming home to beat up his wife."

"That's close, actually," she said. "I never did like intellectuals, or at least the way they relate to their sexuality."

"I don't understand what that means."

"How into this do you want to get now, sweetie?" she said. "How about we just do it and you can hit me if you want to. In fact I think it's kind of sweet and sentimental-"

"It's okay," I said, "I don't have to spank." But halfway into it I did anyway, cupping my hands but hitting her hard.

"That was good," she said afterward. "I mean it really was." Then out of nowhere she embraced me as tightly as I can ever remember. After a minute I could tell she was on the verge of tears.

"I don't want to start up with all of this again, not with you," she said. "I wish you hadn't done that tonight."

"I'm sorry," I said.

"Don't be sorry," she said. "If you're gonna do it, then do it."

Morning came and yellow light spilled through the plastic Venetian blinds into my bedroom. Alexandra left for work about a half-hour earlier than I did, which meant I was always where she wasn't—in bed when she was in the shower, in the shower when she was having coffee in the kitchen, in the kitchen having coffee while she was getting dressed in the bedroom. We'd learned to stay out of each other's hair while we got on with our routines. The morning silence, so absolute, was comforting to both of us. No need for little reassurances and no chance of starting the day off on the wrong foot since both of us were prone to be petty and argumentative in the morning. That morning was no different. I booted up the laptop on the kitchen table and scanned the headlines as I drank my coffee. In the background I could hear her combing her hair and then slipping into one of her business suits, of which she always had one or two hanging in my wardrobe. And then out the door she went with a "see yah."

Later that morning I was at work talking to a client on the telephone. The client, an office manager with a midtown software consulting firm whose lease was set to expire, wanted a two-week extension to give the firm time to move out. I was referring her to the applicable portion of the lease when my instant messenger box popped up on my screen. It was Alexandra.

Call me when you can.

Something weighing on me.

No guts.

I got the client off the phone and without hanging up speed-dialed Alexandra at work.

"I wanted to wait for a better time," she said. "I know I should be saying this in person, but I want to let you know that I haven't forgotten about that conversation we had last night."

"Neither have I," I said.

"I've been seeing someone else for a while. It's a woman. I should have just told you last night."

"Anyone I know?"

"No. She's a specialist."

"A dominatrix," I said.

"She doesn't really have a title but yes, I was lying to you. You see she takes care of those other needs. Does this hurt or what?"

"Like a kick to the kidneys."

"I figured. What do you want to do?"

"Nothing right now," I said. "Let's address this later," and I hung up. I sat there stunned for a few minutes thinking about the bottle of Knob Creek in my bottom drawer. I had a strong urge to get catatonic.

The phone rang again.

"I *am* sorry," she said when I picked it up.

"Did she do the thing with the wooden spoon?"

"She was the one that told me about it in the first place."

"Ouch."

"It would be nice if you could be Teflon man just this once and let it slide," she said. "Maybe give me points for honesty."

"I think not," I said. "But wait, I just want to clarify something. Are you telling me that some dyke does a better job of being a muscled-up pipe-fitter than I do?"

"Hands down. And Joanie's her name, by the way, and she's bi. But believe me, you wouldn't want to be her—she's got her issues. I mean I serve a purpose for *her* as well. You could say our neuroses are perfectly aligned. Not so with you. You shouldn't be taking it personally. I don't love this woman. She serves a purpose."

"And . . . ?"

"Oh and I do love you Curtis, in case you're deaf and blind. I loved you since the first night we went out. Just because I don't want you playing that role doesn't mean I don't love you. It might mean I love you even more."

"I'm going to pour myself some bourbon after I get off the phone with you," but I didn't because the truth was, I was madly in love with Alexandra, always had been. I hung up and took the elevator down to the lobby and walked out onto Sixth Avenue and Fifty-Fourth Street and looked across the broad, senseless avenue. Tourists, taxis, pigeons, delivery trucks, cops. Midtown held no epiphanies for me. The sky was overcast and I could hear a helicopter though couldn't see it. I went back up to my office and read the latest news headlines. I was trying to convince myself that things with Alexandra would work out, that this might add back some of that old excitement. And it was a good test for me—was I adaptable? Did I love her enough to help her work through her issues—if they could even be called issues?

That night, Alexandra and I were sitting across a small table from each other at an Italian restaurant in the East Village. I'd wanted to meet her there with the understanding that this might be our last meal together. She wore her work clothes, a sleeveless black and white gingham dress that rose above her knees. She wore her hair in a flat little bob that was held in place by a shiny metallic clip.

We'd gone through a bottle of verdicchio. A plate of gnocchi sat before her and a plate of spinach penne, before me, both untouched. I couldn't say when the orders had arrived.

". . .and so she—Joanie—would tie you up in this netting?" I said. "Does she prod or whip you?"

"It's much more scientific."

"Does she bring you to orgasm?"

"Sometimes I come, but I have to ask permission. I can't believe I'm getting into the nitty gritty of this with you. It's mostly about pain, not pleasure."

"But I've never seen a mark on you."

"Look at my eyes," and she rolled them so far up that the pupils vanished. There, risen above her lower lids like Antarctica, were duplicate bruises, one on each orb.

"And here," she said, lifting a candle and opening her mouth carefully so that the flickering flame illuminated the inside. Some kind of brand was seared into the pink flesh of one inner cheek. The image of a star, a planet, a spider—I couldn't tell.

"Fuck," I said.

"And I can show you a lot more evidence sometime, if you don't believe me. You don't need so much surface area. All those welts and bruises, it's old school, wasted real estate. I've evolved. You hit the right nerve bundles with the right stimulus, and I swear you get shot to the moon. I mean, it's not *pleasant*. It's not supposed to be. I become nothing in Joanie's hands—a mealy bug, a roach."

"I believe you," I said. I reached across the table for her hand. She took mine and we held onto each other.

"This isn't about my trauma or my sickness," she said. "It's about whether or not you can deal with my habits. I am sorry that I didn't trust you with this stuff. Think of it as a hobby, as something you really needn't have an interest in. Like I have a little room off to the side where I build model airplanes."

"Please," I said. "Don't be an asshole. It's not that simple."

"Don't call me that."

"You like it."

"I like it in the right setting. I love it in the right setting."

"And I'm supposed to know when we're in that setting?"

"Don't be an amateur, Curt. A restaurant is clearly not it. That's your problem, see, your need for reassurance. That vulnerable core of yours begs to be pricked."

Now blood was rising, at last, and that old feeling was coming back on.

"Go into the bathroom," I said, "and come back out with your panties in your purse. *Capiche*?"

"Now's not the time," she said.

"You want to work through this with me? Then return some semblance of control. Don't give it another thought."

She hesitated, then said, "Oh, why not," and she got up and went into the women's room.

I began to eat. The waiter came by and I ordered another bottle of verdicchio.

In a few minutes Alexandra came toward the table. A finger of white fabric stuck out from between her purse clasps, a little flag of compliance. I eyed her chair.

"Sit down."

"As if I'm going to stand here like this."

When she was in place she took my hand again and played with the hair on the back of my fingers. Little strokes, one finger at a time, as if each of my fingers were a dear pet.

"This chair is uncomfortable, you perv'," she said, a smile erupting, imperfect teeth glistening in the candlelight, canines pushed up in front of the rest. Thank god she had never worn braces.

"Did you redo your lipstick in there?"

"Yah."

"Your mouth is sexy."

"It's capable of cruel words."

"I know that."

"For example," she said, "are you aware that while I do love you, I'm not *in* love with you? Not in the least, to be honest. I could make do without you."

"That's a relief," I said. "I'm not particularly in love with you either. Anyway, these things go in cycles."

The wine arrived and the waiter, a tall white guy with no visible tattoos, performed an overpour, as if we were supposed to drink wine like beer. The restaurant should have provided steins instead of stemware if this is the way they wanted to treat us. Alexandra took a gulp and then began eating. She was fully composed, more so than I'd seen her that whole night. I poured a good portion of the wine down my throat and finished what remained on my plate.

When she was about halfway through her gnocchi she stopped short and pointed her fork at me.

"Do you think we should get married?" The question seemed an accusation.

"Are you going to wean yourself from this thing with Joanie?"

"Possibly," she answered.

"Then possibly yes," I said.

"Can you guess the kind of engagement ring I'd like?"

"Something misfitting—too narrow and tight," I said. "Something that draws blood."

"I might be falling back in love with you after all," she said

"It'll be a while before I feel the same way about you," I said, refilling our glasses, and not for the last time.

L.

L. sat at home listening to an audio cassette he'd received from his girlfriend, K., as a farewell—a kind of adieu, see you later but no guarantees, buster, and don't bother trying to find me. He sat alone in the darkness not out of solipsism, but because it was mid-August in New York City and there was a blackout. Naked, L. sat at his desk wearing his Walkman listening to K.'s voice at the lowest possible volume to conserve the batteries, but still he got a certain kick out of it when they finally did begin to die, for she could drone on for so long, and this being her supposedly final message to him, what he imagined would be her pithy observations of his flawed character, the encapsulation of everything she'd imagined they'd meant to each other—for it to be all this and still for her to be going on and on for more than what L. imagined was a half hour—it was funny when the slowing tape turned her voice into a baritone on laughing gas. Then there were only the police and fire and ambulance sirens out on the streets.

"The natives're riotin'" L. said out loud. It was after nine and the sun had left its residue on the horizon, like Popsicle juice around a fat kid's lips, as he saw it. It was hot, damn hot, in his apartment with no current to drive a fan or air conditioner compressor or anything for that matter. No cross breeze either, just one window facing the street, so that he recalled K.'s last recorded words in a thick sweat that stung his eyes. Until the power came back he'd have to keep her words in his mind, swirling them around like cloying grape jelly. "What we had, when we had it right, L., was a good time. You and me can agree on that I think, and I know I learnt a lot from you, what with the museums and the books you lent me I think I've become a better person. And you're a better man for knowing me, too. I taught you more about yourself, made you see the good you have in that good heart of yours. I think, though, that you still don't believe how good you are, which is one more reason I got to leave and do this thing I've always wanted to . . ." Then her voice had started to get stretched out and L. wasn't sure what she was saying, but it didn't matter because the heat was distracting him and he was drinking from a big bottle of beer whose cold he wanted to save from the blackout. He would let nothing go to waste and get as much coolness into his body as possible. After the beer he'd have to drink his milk and then orange juice and then eat his yogurt then the vegetables and citrus fruits including a lemon, which he could do. It was going on pitch-blackness now. What else had K. said? "I'm trustin' you not to tell anybody about my fake I.D.'s and all that jazz." It was just like her, L. thought, to put on tape evidence of her wrongdoing. Though the sun had now vanished, the air seemed to be getting hotter by the minute. Such are the thermodynamic properties of a large city. All that heat energy trapped in the granite, the asphalt, the steel of cars and trucks and busses, the flesh and blood of its residents, all that heat trapped there during the day and radiating into the night. What was it about K. anyway that L. would miss? The sex for one—she was generous in bed, and he was grateful for that. Her insight? Doubtful, she talked with lots of "they shoulda done"s and "the fact of the matter is"s and "ever-wonder-why?"s as though she always knew better, which L. doubted that she did; in fact he thought she was a bit dim upstairs, but very streetwise, which he wasn't, particularly. She'd always said he gave too much money to beggars. "You see a guy, he's missing a tooth, his sneakers are worn through, he's holding a cup out so you jam a dollar bill in it, huh? You're a sucker," she'd say. She never gave a dime or a smile to any stranger on the street. Now she was off to see the country, hitchhiking west with a false name, a new identity, to live some movie script in her head. On the way there she would be buffeted by the interstate winds and her rough-and-tumble experiences on the road—oh, how she hoped to suffer and struggle in the right proportions, how to meet some little-assed, big-shouldered trucker who'd make her feel how L. never could: a bit dirty. This is what L. imagined anyway, to get himself upset. He wondered where she was then, at that moment, and concluded that she was probably just entering Pennsylvania, maybe riding shotgun in one of those new 300 horsepower Nissans, or just the opposite, in an old Caprice with a Pakistani family of six. It didn't matter, she'd be chalking up the experiences while he melted away on the same loveseat he'd first kissed her on. He heard the sound of a breaking shop window out on the street but didn't move for a minute or so. He was five floors up and as he saw it, out of any real danger, other than being poached alive. There'd be looting. He'd figured that. The Starbucks across the street was the one getting it and as he looked out the window and watched a representative mix of his neighborhood's ethnic groups—his own included in that mix—running out with espresso makers and bags of coffee beans and big brass scales and some other machines and utensils that seemed medieval, he couldn't help laughing. There was no irony in it whatsoever, which is what made him laugh. It was the only store without a steel gate and so it was the first store on the block to get looted. K. was out of here and good for her, he thought, out in Pennsylvania, passing through some Dutch-named town, or some town named Some Town as though she were passing through the words themselves. Which was what L. would love to become just then, a word on a piece of paper, any word, to escape the staggering heat, to escape his own heart that was beginning to grow heavy with K.'s absence. He needed to escape the heat in any way possible.

He could hear the sirens getting closer, but sat there on the loveseat, motionless. When the emergency vehicles stopped in front of his building, the strobes making his walls like those of a Mexican discotheque, he ambled over to the window again and watched as a bloodied, shirtless man was strapped onto a gurney and wheeled toward an ambulance. The guy looks like me, L thought, the guy looks exactly like me. He pressed his hands onto his own thighs but there was no tactile sensation, no resistance. The damn heat—numbing, oppressive, hallucinogenic. The man on the gurney was now being administered CPR with a hand pump over his mouth as a second attendant, a slim woman, leaned over his torso. It looked as if she were nursing him. L. could smell her perfume intermingled with the sidewalk trash smell, and the ambulance itself, idling, was putting forth a mini hospital room odor. He was frightened suddenly with a bolt of recognition. His window's security gate was wide open, as was the window, which wasn't so unusual, but so too was the screen. The man on the gurney was now being shut into the ambulance. L. moved onto the fire escape and looked down. A section of the sidewalk was cordoned off with police tape directly below his window. Now he could see a folded note taped to his window, and then he watched as his apartment door opened and a police detective stepped inside. "What's going on?" L. asked. The detective walks past him and removes the note from the windowpane.

"Goddamn heat is making people insane," the detective says to nobody as he gingerly opens the note in an empty apartment.

The Sculptor

If you've heard about me then you know I'm a genius. I've been living down in TriBeCa for almost forty years. Moved in when it was cheap, rats like dogs, industry, no hot water in the loft spaces. But it's my work, my sculptures that you might've read about somewhere. Most recently, *Time* did a little piece on me that included a centerfold of me posing with one of my works; the *Village Voice* did a big spread on me a few years back; *The New Yorker* once in a while reviews—always favorably—my bigger shows, which just about all have been recently. My sculptures have limited lifespans, just like us.

The first sculpture blew itself to bits seven years ago, injured a house cat. The owners were warned. A plaque on its outside stated: LOOK AT ME 2,000 TIMES AND THE 2,001ST TIME I'LL EXPLODE. It worked like a charm. The little papier-mâché ballerina in her clear-resin vitrine, painted hot pink, blue eyes, silver hair made from tin can aluminum turned out, shoes that I'll admit I stole from a doll. There she was upon her small pedestal, and you look at her and the counter—powered by a now-obsolete nickel cadmium battery—records what the motion sensor registers as "a look." At 2,001 I designed the counter to close a circuit and the remaining power from the nick-cad cell fires a small electrical charge that ignites a homemade and quite crude black powder bomb. BOOM! The work goes up up and out out, explodes.

Needless to say that the story, since it was covered in the papers, drew some popular attention to my work. Sculpture with a lifespan. You can't just look at my works nonchalantly—you've got to think about it first. You're more likely to pay attention to the fine detail of the craftsmanship, the ingenuity and subtle symbolism. Of course I suppose if you sat there with binoculars or opera glasses from across the room it wouldn't be registered as a look. But get up close and it will. And with today's equipment and new declassified military technology, a lot more's possible. Maybe I can get my works to register a glance. Hell, a thought.

I've got a lot more works out there just waiting to die. Some, and these are really purely mechanical-based—and here, as far as I know, you can't cheat them—have a shutter that you need to open to see the work at hand. My favorite is the miniature pissing boy, like in Brussels. He's behind a little shutter, or door, and when you open it he turns to you, holding his little kid's penis, and pisses. You've got to keep the little piss reservoir beneath him filled with water, but that's not much work and in no way interferes with the counter. You open the door to take a look at him and an internal sealed mechanism, which is a bit too complicated to explain in a non-technical journal, registers the motion and clicks a counter up by one. When you open this door the 1000th time—and again, my plaque lets you know just how many free looks you get at the pissing boy—the little guy's dissolved away with some dilute hydrochloric acid. The shutter closes, locks, and I imagine you hear a fizzing sound, some bubbling and snapping maybe, and a bit of acrid smoke probably sneaks out. After precisely ninety seconds you're free to open and close the shutters as much as you like, but all that's going to be there is a heap of melted plastic, acrylic and copper leafing.

About a year ago I get a call from Ted Turner. He and Jane are big fans of mine and three years ago he bought one of my most expensive pieces that's got a pretty short lifespan. Five-hundred looks and hydraulic clamps powered by a whole array of batteries crush from all angles a small art-deco style discus thrower with luminous red eyes and a beard that on close inspection is also a serpent. So a year ago Ted calls from his Montana ranch asking me to fly there first class, at his expense of course, to add a couple of hundred looks to his sculpture.

"No can do, sorry Ted," I say. Mr. Turner isn't pleased with this response and offers me an obscene sum of money. Still I say no, and the last I hear, Ted has the thing boxed up and put into storage because he loves it so damn much and knows he only has a few dozen more looks before the fucker gets mashed into a cube and I suppose he wants to save, maybe cherish is a better word, those last looks.

I mention Ted Turner's call to illustrate the temptations I've been put through before. Could be living rich, so flush that I'd be able to buy my nephews and nieces houses with saunas to luxuriate in, myself a second and third home in tropical climes, a studio in each. It'd ruin me, that's for sure, knowing that I sold out.

What, critics have asked, is the drive behind this peculiar artist's works? When I die, they wonder, would not I prefer something to remain of me—does not an artist desire to remain alive in his best works? And through this does he not achieve a sort of immortality? Van Gogh lives! There goes Sylvia Plath! You might feel as though you know them, that a kind of effervescent soulness bubbles from their work; they own a bit of your heart. In my eyes, this sort of "immortality" is shit. Let my obliteration be absolute, let my death be resolute. When I'm gone and my sculptures are gone, let no trace of me remain but a bit of calcium-enriched soil. Let us leave the earth a place scrubbed clean of our presence.

The other day I get a letter from a quite sweet and sexy woman, an heir to a very prominent New York family. Not as rich as Ted Turner, but a hell of a lot better looking. Old money, real estate, that kind of stuff. In the letter she reminds me of the piece she bought a few years back and invites me over for tea. Wonderful! I think. Here's some real class and I love being civilized and am always looking for a reason to shave, get a haircut and scrub with some exfoliant. So I take a subway uptown, walk to Sutton Place and go to the second floor of a brownstone that she owns, and she greets me in negligee! I like this, I think. It's been too long for me. Being somewhat past my prime in matters of lust, I was immediately grateful to know that everything was working.

"Come in, why don't you?" she says, sauntering to a leather sofa and marble-topped coffee table where she has prepared tea and biscuits. My sculpture is in the background, dual-lighted with recessed halogen spots, and I go to inspect it. "Oh no!" she shouts, "Please don't look. Not much time left for him, I'm sorry to say. Anyway, that's why I've called you here. I'm hoping I can have you, y'know, fix it so that I'll have more time with him."

I tell her I don't do that, and then I pour us some tea.

"Surely," she says, raising her eyebrows and crossing her legs daintily, but so that I can get a little look at what she's trying to show me, "you can make an exception with me?"

"Can't," I say. Tea's Earl Grey, good stuff, though I find caffeine aggravates my prostate condition.

"Another day," she says, "two maybe, tops, and that wonderful work you've made specifically for me, the pure masculine centerpiece of my life, will be gone, burned alive in this very room. Surely you can help me. There's no price too steep for me. I've money and anything or everything else you could possibly want."

"Lady," I say, "I'm sure grateful for what you're trying to do for me, and god knows I can use a little, a taste or touch, but you see, I can't be bought. If you'd like to commission me to make a new one, similar to but not a duplicate of this one, with more sophisticated sensors and destructive devices, I'd be glad to. And I'm interested in whatever you've got to barter with, but this bastard, as far as I'm concerned, is dead." She begins to weep, gets up, and walks into her bedroom. I sit back in the plush sofa and have another biscuit. In a couple of minutes she emerges wearing a neck-to-toe robe and looks a little embarrassed with herself. She walks me to the door, kisses me wetly on the lips, and says she'll think about my proposition.

I'm recalling this anecdote to illustrate the suffering I'm put through at times. Believe me, I'd love some of what she was offering. But once an artist's integrity goes, so goes his craft.

Most recently I've been working on an interpretive self-portrait. It is a rather hirsute man of Latin American heritage, somewhat below average height. His posture is good, chin held up pridefully in the manner of his people, spine straight. He is, in fact, me, and I'm wearing what appears to be a black felt fedora replete with an imitation feather and a red nylon band running around the crown. How is this a work of art? My "hat" will be a counting instrument of the previously-described highly sophisticated type. It will count glances until the one hundredth person takes a gander at the ugly thing. Then an illegally purchased charge of C4 will obliterate my cranium. Look at me too much, give me too much of your attention, and you'll no longer have me around to appreciate. Look upon things carefully, with your full consideration, for everything has its lifespan. Save your nonchalant, careless, daydreamy half-stares for television. Be observant. And when it comes to art and people, pull that precision lens over your visual cortex. Take it all in, especially that old man wearing the ugly fedora. You'll never see another exactly like him.

Lemon

It's the winter of 1992 and Lemon walks past the travel agency on his block. I'm not supposed to be thinking about travel, he thinks. Should be thinking about staying right here, for a long time. Forever. Don't think about the warm waves lapping at your naked toes during sunset, or margaritas on that same beach, or even girls. First approached the travel agency then was in front of it, looked into it, saw posters of Rio De Janeiro, Cancun, ancient Mayan ruins—posters that he didn't remember seeing last time—and this is when he thought those thoughts. Mustn't, he thinks. No use, can't help wanting to leave.

It begins to snow, wet and heavy. The streets glimmer. It's two P.M. and the sun is hidden behind the clouds, and the snow begins to move along in waves well above him, even above the taller office buildings along the avenue. The sun, he thinks, yes, its radiating warmth on the beach, and girls there too, in bikinis, and me with so much money that I'd be flush forever, no matter what I bought—mansions, sports cars, finest wines. And money to spare for horses, stables for the horses, a farm where wool from my own sheep would be shorn and woven into sweaters for my family, just the wife and daughter if we didn't want any more children, and I'd never kill an animal; they'd all happily give milk or whatever they give and in the end die of natural causes. Never a shot fired unless it was to put an old beast out of its misery or to ward off an intruder.

Lemon's pants are torn and he can feel moist air and a few wet snow flakes falling down one of his legs. He likes the feeling. Turns, goes three more blocks to a peep show in Times Square, hangs his head low, shuffles past the attendant, finds an empty booth, takes out a roll of singles, puts several into the machine, sits. A curtain opens and a light-skinned black woman, maybe late-thirties, around Lemon's age, stands behind a thick, dirty Lexan pane.

"Hey there baby," she says. Her voice crackles through a little speaker protected by steel mesh. The sound comes out between his knees. Bright light shining on her, Lemon hidden in the shadows, hand in the single pant hole, groping himself. "What do you want me to do for you, hon'?" the woman says, removing a pink teddy then squatting on the floor close to the transparent plastic window. She's topless now but wearing panties and an old pair of cowboy boots.

"Usual," Lemon says, "whatever's usual."

"Nothing's usual anymore. Everyone's got their things, their proclivities. C'mon," she says, "who am I? Mom, Sis, next store neighbor?"

"How about a stripper," Lemon says, "in a goddamned box."

"You got that right," she says.

Lemon asks the woman to remove the rest of her clothing and stand back so he can see all of her.

"You want to talk to me?" she asks. "You want me to say nasty things: suck, fuck, blowjob, cum?"

"No," Lemon says, "just let me see you." He looks at her for a while, the curtain begins to close, puts in more dollars, watches her until the curtains close again, then leaves. Can't get the smell of the disinfectant from the booth out of his nose. Keeps snorting, blowing out of his nostrils. A little snot comes out and he wipes it off with the back of his jacket sleeve.

When he's a block away from the peep show he sees his daughter, who's eleven years old, walking toward their apartment on the other side of the street. He crosses, catches up to her.

"Tara," he shouts, but she's wearing her headphones. So he taps her on the shoulder and turns her. She lets out a little yelp. "Shouldn't you be in school now?" he says.

"They sent me home because I'm sick, Dad. I called you first but there was no answer. So I walked."

"They let you walk all this way," Lemon says, "even though you're sick?"

"Yes, Dad. Swollen glands. They said 'Go home,' so I did. I know the way just fine." Lemon places a hand under his daughter's chin and feels around. "Ow!" she says when he touches a tender lump.

"Feels swollen to me, too. Let's get you home and in bed. I'll pick up some chicken soup."

He walks her back to the apartment, stopping at a Polish diner for soup to go, then up their six flights of steps. Inside he sees that she puts on sweats—which double as her pajamas—and gets under the blankets. He brings her the soup and sits next to her on the bed. She lets him feed her a few spoonfuls of soup then insists on doing it herself. He touches her forehead. "Fever, maybe. I'm calling the doctor. Let him comfort me, or let him drop by as long as he doesn't charge an arm and a leg.

"Be careful with the soup, don't spill any on the blankets. It'd stink them up before anybody knew they should be washed."

He calls the doctor. "Could be the mumps," the doctor says over the phone, "but she was inoculated, so her records say. Probably nothing to worry about. The flu maybe, or a low-grade infection of some kind. Kids' immune systems are quite responsive to any kind of pathogen. Keep an eye on her and take her temperature. If it's higher than 102, call me back. I'll call the pharmacist—where do you live again?—and you can pick up some good strong medicine for her. Help her sleep, which is really the most important thing. Let her body do most of the work. What's your plan again?"

"We're not covered anymore," Lemon says. "Lost my job a few months back. Judy cleans apartments. No coverage."

The doctor pauses on the other end. "I'll specify generic," he says. "I'll make sure they've got it. That'll save you some money.

I also won't charge you for the call or anything, for that matter, until you get some coverage."

"Thanks," Lemon says, "there aren't many like you around these days," he adds.

The doctor says, "I went into the business to help families raise healthy children. I've got a big practice and right now money's no problem. That's bound to change, of course."

"Well thanks, Doc," Lemon says, and hangs up.

He looks down at his pants and thinks about the peep show woman. Her breasts were uneven, which he knows is natural but somehow didn't expect. Her bush was big and glistened—it's in the nature of pubic hair, he thinks, wondering if that's right. Maybe just the bright lights. A nice smile though, but a tooth that was clearly false—different color than the rest.

"Daddy," his daughter cries from the other room, "I spilled a little soup."

"Shit. Okay, we'll deal with it when your mother comes home."

He thinks about the peep show woman for five more minutes, decides she was flawed in a number of ways. Then he tells his daughter he'll be back in a little while, that he's got to pick up her prescription. It's a few blocks away, he says, and he goes out with a full roll of quarters and some loose bills in the other pocket.

Goes into another peep show place, this one with movies, cheaper. Sits in a booth, same stink of disinfectant. A small screen in front of him. 50 CENTS = 3 MINUTES, a sign reads above it. He places four quarters into the machine. The screen comes alive, flickers. Two men, boys really—must be seventeen, Lemon thinks—having sex by a swimming pool. Lemon uses the control next to the coin slot to change the channel. A woman performing fellatio. Lemon watches, gropes himself a little. Changes the channel. A woman and man watching each other masturbate. Bright studio lights shine on them and Lemon can see the glare from their pallid skin. He concludes that they don't eat enough vegetables and fruits, or are pale from sedentary lifestyles, or from drugs. Doesn't see any tracks on their arms, but that can be hidden with makeup and these days you don't need to use a needle to be an addict. Changes the channel. A black woman and a white man—the screen goes blank. Inserts six more quarters, screen flickers on again. The black woman straddles the white man as he lies on a small single bed. Looks like a hotel or motel room, Lemon thinks. Isn't usually attracted to black women, but this one is sweet-looking, has straightened her hair as he likes, shaved her pubic area, and the man's not so big. Changes the channel. An orgy.

He tries to see what the people look like, tries to identify whom the two legs closest to the camera belong to. Then there's a close-up of a man performing cunnilingus. He breaks away, winks at the camera, Lemon laughs, the man resumes, Lemon changes the channel then the screen goes blank again. He leaves, goes three more blocks, picks up his daughter's prescription, walks back, goes up the steps, comes inside.

She's asleep. The television is on a cable station that only shows cartoons. He sits beside her, reads the directions on the bottle of cough medicine, and watches cartoons. His daughter turns in her sleep so that she's on her back. Lemon gently presses his lips onto her forehead. She's still warm, he thinks, but not so much that I should worry. And anyway, she's sleeping. He turns the television off and goes into the kitchen.

He takes chicken livers out of the freezer and puts them into the microwave to defrost, cuts up a Spanish onion, takes his daughter's unfinished chicken soup from the bedroom and puts it in a pot on the stove to keep it warm. Takes butter from the fridge, puts it in a pan, throws in the diced onion, defrosted liver, boils water for rice. Then his wife comes home. "Tara's sick," he tells her. "They sent her home from school early. She's been sleeping okay though. Low-grade fever, but I called the doctor and he prescribed some cough medicine which is on the night stand."

He watches as his wife does exactly what he did: presses her lips against their child's forehead and comes away not too concerned.

"Liver again?" she asks.

"I was meaning to go out and get some broccoli and garlic and stuff, maybe even some pignoli nuts. Thought that I could make pasta primavera, throw the nuts under the broiler to brown them first, like you like it. But Tara being sick and my having to get the medicine and all, I didn't have time to do it."

"It's okay," his wife says, kissing him on the cheek. "What a shitty day though. Scrubbing toilets and bathtubs, shower stalls, bringing curtains to the dry cleaners, even changing a cat box and then, just now, coming home, telling the guy around the corner to back off for asking me for money. 'You give *me* some,' I wanted to say. I'd like to get out of this neighborhood. When you find work we'll have enough to move. No reason to stay where we are. So close to all that dirt and filth. It's not even such a great deal, rent-wise."

"The thing I like about it," Lemon says, "is the dollar-fifty theater across the street. They have some good movies too. There's that new James Bond flick there now. We should take advantage of it more."

"How can we?" she says. "Last time we went all the riffraff made such a racket that I couldn't hear a thing and then Tara started crying and we got screamed at and had to leave."

"We could get a baby sitter and go by ourselves," Lemon says.

"That's a joke," his wife laughs, "right? Because you know we have no money."

"Mommy!" comes from the other room, and she goes to her daughter.

Later in the week his wife's working and daughter at school and Lemon walks past the travel agency without looking in, feels the fresh bills in his pocket, and goes into a newly-opened peep show. Bright pink awning, neon outline of a woman—her breasts and hips curvaceous—on the front. Head down, Lemon pays the attendant to get in, is walked to a booth by a middle-aged bleached blonde—she waits for a tip, he gives her a dollar—and sits down in a new chair. A flimsy door closes behind him. No smelly disinfectants. An illuminated liquid crystal display in front of him says that his twenty dollar entrance fee has bought him ten minutes, but that an additional ten dollars at any time will buy him another ten. A black curtain opens and behind the divider—

Lemon notices that it's not plastic but glass and very clean and not scratched anywhere—is a young woman, maybe twenty-one or -two, who looks like she's still in college. Doesn't know exactly why he thinks she's in college, maybe something alive in her eyes or very intelligent in the way she holds herself, her good posture.

Her hair is long, light brown, and in a ponytail bound with a rubber band. She's wearing a t-shirt and blue jeans. She smiles at him, or where he supposes she supposes he resides in the shadows behind the glass divider, and begins to undress. He edges forward in the chair, hands at his side. She moves closer to the glass divider and begins to gyrate awkwardly, self-consciously, as she removes her clothing.

It's her first time, he thinks. Poor girl's never done this before. She stops looking in his direction, instead looks up somewhere just above him, vacantly, into space. Lemon figures that she's thinking nothing, that she's partly leaving her body. He looks closely at her skin, at its new, almost baby smoothness. Her navel is neatly tweaked into her belly like a very small flower. Now naked, she rotates, holds her hands above her head, comes back around to face the glass divider, begins to spin faster, as a dancer might, straightens her toes, legs taut, belly flattening, a slight crimson flush above her breasts and in her cheeks.

She takes the classical stand of a ballerina, as Lemon has not seen since his mother used to take such classes when he was ten and eleven years old. She used to practice late into the night. He'd sneak downstairs, watch his father watching his mother from the living room Recline-o-matic, her dancing for him in her house dress, barefooted, head upright, neck straight, father smoking a cigar. Just like it, only Mother was smiling, would collapse in Father's lap when she was through and occasionally laugh and then Lemon would run up to his room.

His breath leaves a small smudge of condensate as he watches the dancer. Then the curtain begins to close. He grabs for the bills in his pocket but hesitates. In the polished glass he sees his reflection, the blush of excitement, the sweat beaded around his lips, the way his pupils have dilated. He slips two fives into the machine and the curtains open, taking his reflection with them. She starts to dance again, and Lemon watches her dance until all his money is gone.

The Seep

For several months I see my name etched in the sidewalk concrete of the city I've recently moved to. At first I can ignore it but after a while I think there's somebody else with my name who's well known, or a gangster or street kid who's marking territory. I admit it's odd, as my name is somewhat unusual, but it's all I can think of. Somehow he's managed to get his name—my name—into the sidewalk concrete in several seemingly random locations. But soon my name seems to be proliferating. I continue to rationalize it as a coincidence of some sort and even think that I'm blowing things out of proportion. Things are not going so smoothly for me after all; I haven't yet been able to get into the swing of my new job and my apartment faces an alleyway where almost no light penetrates and I have this feeling of dread that things here just won't work out. And then one Saturday morning, early as I go out for a run, there's my name, etched in a similar hand as the rest—a neat, gothic script—in a freshly cured panel of concrete at the foot of my building's stoop. What—? How—? I think. No, now this is too much. In the evening I call an old girlfriend who's been living in this city for several years.

"You would think that these people—what do you call people who do that to wet concrete?—are interested in you," she says. "You always did think that you were the focus of a hidden conspiracy. But come now, what's the real reason you called? And I should let you know that I'm happily engaged to a wonderful, self-assured man with a solid career and all the necessary child-rearing attributes that most men are lacking these days."

"No, really," I say, "just wondering if you've seen anything like this before, or heard of somebody who's noticed a similar pattern with his or her name." Maybe, I think, it's just some bizarre feature of the city.

"Never," she says, "though it does sound like a nightmare I used to have but haven't since a heavy dose of analysis and the wonderful man I've mentioned."

"Well okay," I say, "in the dream, what happens? I mean, sounds ridiculous, but it's all I've got to go on now. And maybe it is nothing at all, but this morning the name appeared in front of my building in fresh concrete."

"That is strange I'll admit, but most likely nothing more than your own paranoia coupled with coincidence."

"But the dream," I say, "tell me about the dream."

"Yes. In it I'm young, nineteen or twenty, the same age as when you and I first met, only I'm in a different city, one I'd never been to in reality, or, rather, that I'm not sure even exists in reality. I'm alone mostly for very long periods of time, almost like a strange kind of punishment, or solitary confinement with the auspices of a real, functional life. I begin to notice my three initials hand-painted on a few walls here and there. At first I think nothing of it, but then I see it more often and sometimes larger letters as well, scrawled across entire facades of buildings in bright hues of fuchsia and a kind of lively candy pink. Quite vivid colors for a dream. Soon the initials are everywhere—I mean everywhere I turn, on every surface, and I begin to spin and spin and spin and the entire city folds in around me until I am suffocated by it. I always awoke in a cold sweat, a dizzying state of fright and for a few moments my room spun about me." Her voice trails off and there's a pause.

"Frightening," I say, sounding some concern, "but did you ever find out who or what was painting your initials? Did you ever solve that little mystery?"

"It's a dream so what do you think? I was responsible for the entire thing, or 'I' as in 'my subconscious.' The only mystery was what the dream revealed and that my very good Austrian analyst and I decided was, among a myriad of extremely complex phobias, an overwhelming urge to find my own identity, that is, what lay beneath my various facades, while at the same time a fear of what might be discovered. Fascinating dream though, don't you think?"

"Er, yes, I suppose. But you see to me it's no dream. You understand? This is really happening to me."

"Of course it is," she says calmly, "but sometimes, if we're desperate enough, dream-like symbolisms can leak through to reality, you understand?"

"Yes," I say, "you mean we hallucinate."

"Yes and no. Sometimes our dreams manifest themselves physically, in actuality, that is—oh, do you hear that? That baritone 'hello my love' you just heard in the background is my sweetheart returning home from his job at the Exchange. I should say goodbye now."

"Thanks, I suppose," I say, discouraged.

"Certainly let me know how things develop," she says. "It's all so interesting, things of this sort, and I'll be sure to mention it to Leopold to get his interpretation."

"Please don't," I say.

"As you wish," and we say goodbye to each other.

I'm still dumbfounded as to the origins of the name that appears to be intended for me in the sidewalks of my new city. For several more days I walk the streets in search of a clue. For a short time I am relieved that no more names appear and I get to thinking about what my ex-girlfriend said about the dream-like manifestations of the subconscious, or was it the unconscious I wonder, how they can find their way into our reality, can punch a hole right into the here and now and slowly seep in, changing our world.

So I wander alone and remain that way through the course of most days and nights for several weeks. After I've had my job for some time I form some good professional friendships. I'm in the numbers business. That is I'm an analyst that depends—our company depends—heavily on all kinds of sophisticated statistical analyses of the markets and weather and various fads that affect the financing of other major fads and athletic teams and automotive unions as well as the publishing industry and advertising rates and how the national psyche is understood overseas and then again how that understanding translates into fluctuations not only in the yen and the pound and the mark, but also into the net worth of international portions of domestic businesses that have a dependence on a specific currency, and how once again a fluctuation in that currency reflects back to us here in the office and indicates, in the end, how well we have predicted it all. I've got a good reputation as somebody who has a sense of how this all works and so have gained the respect of many of my coworkers and supervisors. It's all like a giant engine, I tell them. Pistons, a crankshaft, gasoline mixed with air and ignited, a timing chain, valves, spark plugs, etcetera, and all to drive a set of wheels. So yes, I develop a friendship with one particular woman and one night it turns past friendship into an affair, though brief, and then several months later into a regular, predictable and always enjoyable union. She moves in. Her name's Maxine.

Late one night we're lying in bed, both smoking cigarettes. "I'll teach you how to make love to me even better," she says. "I want you to help me achieve multiple-multiple orgasms." She hands me a study done at a major university. Sketches of generic-looking people involved in coitus of varying degrees of complex athletic flexibility and agility. There's lots of small print about frequency of thrusts, depths of penetration, simultaneous stimulation of various anatomical features and erogenous zones, many of which I did not at first know by name. We try it a few times. It takes a long time to figure out exactly what to do, but we lay the book open on the bed and get down to it. In the end I fail at the endeavor, and Maxine leaves me. Soon she is transferred to Bermuda to set up a captive insurer for a major oil company and I never hear from her again.

Alone in the evenings, I once again look for my name in the sidewalks around town. To my delight and dread, there are several new sightings the first night. The neat script is nearly the same each time, the initial K of my name with its tails and swirls and other frills, the letters that follow neat and cold and lacking the panache of the over-sized K. I make a stenciling of one of the engravings and hang it on the best lighted wall of the apartment. I buy a large survey map of the city and mark all the sightings on it with red thumbtacks. Using a similar but smaller map as a guide, I traverse streets and sidewalks on the other side of town, through slums and working-class neighborhoods, the manufacturing district and ethnic enclaves looking for my name. Every time I make a new sighting I mark it on the small map and at the end of the night, or very early the next morning, I return home and transfer the night's catch to the larger map. After months of doing this I exhaust every city street and alley and am finally satisfied that I've documented all the inscriptions. There are 112 in all. As a result of the long hours every night I spend hunched over and staring down at the city's sidewalks, I'm falling behind noticeably at work because I'm just too tired to plug away at the emulation models we use, too exhausted to do even the simplest financial projections. And, well, my mind's loose inside, stars at the fringes of my eyesight, and a petulant, high-pitched ringing in my ears all the time.

I rest up and begin to recover my faculties. One night I stay late at the office, so late that everybody's left. The only light in the place is the green phosphorescence of my computer screen. I stay because I'm finally able to make some progress on a problem that's been baffling my coworkers for weeks. My love of work is beginning to return! I think to myself as I jot down some differential equations on my office pad. Suddenly I have a feeling that there's somebody behind me, a little raspy breathing, the rustle of clothing. I swivel around on my chair. Standing in the shadows—which in such darkness are absolute—is a dward. What's a dward? One who is stern, adheres to his own laws without deviation, will in fact murder you to keep to the rules he's made for himself. This one I felt I knew, somehow knew. "All those symbols must get confusing," he says slowly from the darkness, a finger coming into the dull light and pointing to the office pad. His voice is like a finer grade of sandpaper. "You know, I could never get myself to go so deeply into mathematics. It seems such a bore, such a bore indeed. But you, well, just look at all that scrawl." He steps out of the blackness toward me. His glasses glint and I see what I think is a smile on his wan face. This dward, whose name eludes me, comes into the light and I see that, yes, he is smiling, a short, filed-tooth smile of bad dentistry or torture. A cheap cologne sweetness wafts over me, but I know it is his odor, the scent of nervousness and fear. A dward's defense against his countless enemies is to smell sweet during times of crisis—to hide beneath a veil of cloying sweetness—as this one, vaguely familiar to me, does now. "I must congratulate you on your detective work," he says, taking out a cigarette and tapping it on the fine fabric of his overcoat. "You've beautifully displayed contemporary man's ability for obsessiveness. Really, I am impressed, going into such bad neighborhoods by yourself, risking life and no doubt limbs to chase—well really, to chase what? Some sidewalk graffiti? And do you now feel relieved? Was it cathartic for you too?" He laughs quietly, lights the cigarette.

I'm working late, having some success with a problem my coworkers have not been able to solve when I hear something, somebody, behind me. I swivel around in my chair and start because I think I see someone standing in the dark shadows. But no, I'm wrong. It's just my raincoat on the coat rack. Just in case, I turn on all the office lights. It's very bright now and I continue to work until about two in the morning, finally solving the problem and tying it up into one succinct set of equations. Satisfied, gleeful in fact, I turn the lights off, lock up the office, and get into a waiting taxi outside.

I Am an Actuary

People often ask me what actuaries do. I say that they entrench themselves in bunkers made of paper. Computer-generated reports are the walls of the bunker. We drink coffee inside them and manage to announce things such as impending marriages and the birth of our children via an intercom system. We have data slides wherein yards of paper collapse upon a fellow analyst. Sometimes, but not very often, an actuary is crushed to death. Last time was August of 1986 when Jerome Naas died. His bunker was cleaned out, the walls taken away, and his space given to me. I've made certain that the base of my walls are thick and stable—as they get taller, this is quite important. People still refer to my bunker as Jerome's.

In the printer room paper is fed into an IBM 4085 series IV printer. It works constantly—all night and day—and heats the room to an unbearable temperature. The Paper Sergeant makes sure that the paper gets distributed, that the reports are as per the requested specifications, and that the actuarial systems programmer responsible for running the job is around to give it a once over. Physically, reports are distributed by Joseph, the forklift driver. Bunker walls become taller and thicker. Inside, the actuary shouts thanks for the report, says he'll (or she'll) look at it soon. Requests are generated constantly for fear that the sheer volume of paper distributed will dwindle. "We're a growth industry," my boss always says.

Denise comes by to check on me sometimes. She's the best manager the office has had. If I'm tired she'll bring me coffee; if out of supplies, she'll have them delivered; if lonely, we'll make love. She's not tall and blond, no blue eyes, no pert ears and perfectly arched nose. She's dark, has deep brown eyes, steel thighs, calves of stone, lips arched and defined, black hair braided with silver beads.

I have a single, yellowish fluorescent bulb overhead that buzzes as it flickers. The last time I looked in a mirror (my last vacation—155 weeks ago?) I was jaundiced. The whites of my eyes were speckled with layers of livered yellow. I'm lucky though. I've been told by Denise that my teeth are the best in the office. I brush twice daily and floss. Beneath my credenza are my sanitary facilities: a small shower and sink and a toilet. A thick oak trapdoor opens onto it and I descend four steps, as if into a windjammer's hull, and crouch to do whatever my business is, or stand to shower. It's also where Denise and I go, she bending over the toilet and I, jammed between her and the sink, leaning over her bare back. The smooth line of her spine runs into me like a runway. Coming in for a landing. She groans at the toilet tank and I groan into her ear. Her silver-beaded braids clank against the cold porcelain.

I get carried away sometimes and she has to stop me. But Denise comes back, always, and looks toward the credenza. There's no missing that look, and it's usually exactly what I need as well. I envy her. "When you leave here," I ask, "where do you go?" "Home," she says. "Queens. I pick up groceries on the way, cook dinner for my kids. You know, just what you'd expect." "I have no expectations," I say. We're both naked as we chat, and the little room smells like what I remember the Maine coast to smell like. Only sweeter, with the scent of pines or fir trees drifting down to the beach to mingle with the sea-weed smell of the tidal zone. "Aren't you married?" I ask. I always ask this question to reiterate that what we sometimes do is edged with danger. She goes along. "Yeah. Reginald. He's gone to Corsica again." "Oh. How long?" "A week," she says, "maybe two." She gets dressed and I'm sorry to see the only brightness of my day cover herself up in pantyhose and a little brazier, a simple flowered blouse and a slick looking blue pants suit. "Can I take all of that off you again, just for the hell of it?" I ask. "I've got to go," she says. "Maybe later." "Yes. Come back later," I say. "Maybe," she says, and vanishes up the small staircase, lifting the thick door. I never help her leave.

I just stand there taking in the scent. Then I get dressed. I think about what her husband is missing. My phone rings—quick, single rings, an internal call—and I rush up the steps, bang my head on the hatch door, and manage to grab the receiver before the phone rings a fourth time. "G.D. bloody hell Edwards, where have you been?" yells my boss. "How many G.D. rings does it take for you to get off your lazy butt? I need the net present value report delivered to me immediately. Did you check it?" "Yes," I say, lying. "I'm sending Romeo over now to pick it up," he says, the last words cut off as he hangs up. I imagine him slamming his fist down on the call light and petite Romeo, our Filipino messenger, appearing before the light has even blinked twice, his dark eyes dilated with eagerness, his black hair slicked back with gel. I imagine further what my boss says: "Pick up a report from Edwards, cubicle eighty-one, Jerome's old bunker, and send Trevor over there to check on his report count. His requests are down." Not that there could be much to argue with here. I am in cubicle eighty-one and my requests are down by approximately twelve percent. Romeo will sprint full speed and, like a steeple chaser, make his way to me, bounding over any obstacle.

Steeple chase. How do I know what that is? Yes, a past. High school! I remember now: Rosemary Donaldson and I sitting on a steeple chase beam at one in the morning French kissing under a blank sky, fumbling with our hands, our tongues colliding. After a minute or two we detach. "What is this?" she asks, looking at what we are sitting on. "A steeple chase beam," I answer. "There's a better name for it, but I only know it as a steeple chase beam. They jump up and over it during the race. And what's this?" I ask. "That's my bra," she says, "and you'd better lay off it." Her breasts, my god. We never did do it. We were too frightened. This memory takes me to my home, to the house I grew up in, and my mother cooking borscht in a large pot, the smell of it infusing the house and staying in the bed sheets and pillowcases for days afterward.

Romeo arrives and with two outstretched arms I hand him the report, which is about two-thousand pages. He heaves it onto his shoulder, but it's too tall, not stable enough, and it unravels onto the floor. Tears rise to my eyes as I contemplate the unordered jumble of paper on the floor. Just then Denise comes by and sees what has happened. We begin to pick up the pages. They are numbered.

Aesthetic Displeasure Unearths Lack of Marital Fortitude

Don and Tanya's weekend house, a restored Victorian in Callicoon, NY, sits on a high hill above the Delaware River. It was late, a winter night, and the river, discernable under moonlight, sparkled in the valley below like a giant S. I pulled into their big driveway and turned off the ignition on my old Plymouth Horizon, which ran on for a few strokes. Don, bearded, met me at the front door of the house and led me into the foyer with a big hand on my shoulder. I took my boots off. No heat in the car meant this was not an easy task. As I was hard at work shimmying them off, I noticed a brand new Husqvarna chainsaw sitting there on a little table in plain site. It was quaintly frosted with sawdust upon its bar and chain. The sawdust, to my eye, seemed suspiciously fine, of the circular saw or jigsaw variety, not of the course type that a chainsaw produces.

Inside, Don's old college friends (I'm one) and friends from the couple's dating years in the East Village stood on the periphery of the large living room. Tanya owns a profitable interior design firm in Chelsea, and her clientele milled about the core of the room. This latter group seemed to be in their element, intermixing with ease, speaking with hushed tones, emoting with murmurous laughter and the occasional italicized syllable. A Christmas tree—as waifish as a fashion model—stood in one corner. A brass menorah was perched on the mantel, all the candles lit despite the holiday having progressed only to day two.

Don, standing next to me in jeans with work gloves sticking out of the pockets, pointed out that rarely spotted though somewhat dully colored creature—the chief actuary. This one, Ace Fredrickstoon, ~ of New York Midland Insurance Companies, kept his right hand resting on his left palm and seemed to be deftly performing calculations with both sets of fingers simultaneously, as if working up some exquisite loss expectation for the night. Toward the core of the group, a well-known hedge fund manager wore a cheap Timex and his shirt collar was worn through; and there by the fire was the semi-famous botanist (he'd recently had a paper in *Nature* regarding cycads and fruit bats and dementia in Guam) who, later in the night, would amuse us all by theatrically refusing the green salad; the construction contractor, who was under investigation for using substandard concrete on a job involving a new high school in New York City, wore a cravat emblazoned with back hos.

An ample supply of wood was stacked beside the hearth: maple, oak, even apple and cherry. The stack had the feel of a giant basket of potpourri, more display and scent than fuel. That, along with the chainsaw sitting there in the foyer in obvious display and Don's new outdoorsy look, made me suspect that Tanya was micromanaging their image. Her clients were people that might spend hundreds of thousands of dollars on interior decor without hesitation—that is, once they learned to trust their interior designer. So I couldn't really blame her for wanting to generate a certain rustic feel to the restored home, to beguile them with hardscrabble nuances like the "utilized" chainsaw and the woodsman husband.

"You see that one over there?" Don said, indicating a woman sitting alone on a Shaker chair close to the fire, her back to us. She was reading one of the strategically placed magazines on country décor or organic style or masonry stoves. Twin braids of blond hair snaked down her shoulders and over the back of the chair, where they hung there in stiff suspension. "Lara Whiddon," Don said, "widowed by a hot-shot corporate attorney. Wealthy. Greenwich. He took his motorcycle out for a spin one afternoon about six months ago and never came back. They found his body in a cow pasture about thirty feet from a smashed-in guardrail. His bike was in a hundred pieces and his body wasn't in much better shape."

"Sadness ensued," I said.

"Thing is, he and Lara had just announced their impending divorce. They'd been having trouble for a while and wanted to let everyone know that the split was amicable. She didn't want any of us to feel we had to walk on eggshells around them—there was no need to pretend none of this was happening. 'Because,' she said to Tanya, 'it *is* happening.' That kind of honesty—how can you not admire it? It's pure class."

"How's she holding up?" I said.

"Not great. You see the road he crashed on was one of his favorites. Knew it like the back of his hand. So you can imagine what she thought."

"Suicide," I said.

"Something less explicit," and you could see him think for a few seconds. "Distraughticide," he said. "He was upset and probably blowing off steam out on that road, riding like a daredevil."

I watched her as she put down what she'd been reading and tried to get a hold of a little tabby that had been making the rounds, rubbing against every chair, table and human leg in sight then trotting off when touched as if stunned by such untoward behavior. Like everyone else, she failed to nab the little cat. Then she turned around and surveyed the place for a minute. She wore no makeup and was very pale, her dark eyebrows thick and unplucked, nearly meeting in the center, and you could see that without any effort at all she was a beautiful woman, though beautiful in a way that wasn't fashionable. Her features were plain and clean and broad, her hair pulled back and parted roughly in the center, as if done out of utility. Don gave her a little half-wave when she looked our way. She smiled at us without opening her mouth and then quickly returned to her reading.

"She showed up but I guess she doesn't want to mix," he said. "And how can you blame her? Look at this crowd. Tanya's friends. I don't know sometimes what the hell I'm doing here. It's a show, you know that?"

"Sure," I said. "But she's got a booming business so I guess sometimes you've got to play along, do your part." Truth was, I was just a tad jealous of their material riches, all the fine booze and food, all that space the house provided, the opportunity to be careless, and I imagined that if the place were mine I'd be lying around naked in front of the fire sipping cognac all weekend.

"Yeah. I've got to play along like another prop in her production. I'm supposed to be able to halve a dime with an axe and brawl like a quarryman. But truth is I'm timid as a mouse, you know that. Tanya and I go to some of these local bars to get acculturated, so that she can absorb the 'American ethos,' which of course means absorb it ironically. We walk in and some of these men look at me like I'm a faggot and they look at Tanya like a piece of meat. They've been in the quarry or mill, working bluestone all day and we walk in all fake and scrubbed clean."

"Throwing yourself to the lions," I said. "You get a sense of how to handle yourself."

"I'm thirty-five years old and don't care about being a tough guy. There's no need for it," he said. "The only advantage is picking up on the weird rumors that get going around here."

"Like what?" I said.

"Jesus. Well we got the old mountain lion story that just won't die. That a big cat is leaving calf carcasses up in the trees. It seems they do that out west; go kill a calf then put it high up where nothing else can get a hold of it. Come back for it when they're good and hungry. So we got people saying dairy farmers keep finding their dead calves thirty feet up in some tree limb, but whenever you try to find the farmer, to track down the actual story, it vanishes. Then we recently heard that a group of coyotes had attacked some canoers on the river early one morning. This New Jersey family had come ashore in Long Eddy in two boats, down at a little beach. They planned on having a big fry-up on an open fire, but then a pack of coyotes attacked them and got their food. The whole family—little kids included—jumped back into the river, where they just barely made it into one canoe without paddles and rode the river down to Hankins. They came ashore bruised up and scared, the dear little children still bawling. But then, shortly after that, nobody could name the family or find either canoe or the coyotes. You get it—you can never actually find the source." But he wasn't done yet. "The newest rumor is that there's a robot on the loose, some escaped prototype from a lab outside of Hancock, a converted railroad switch factory owned by Bell Labs, they say. So this thing—I love this one—somehow escaped the facility and is out and about, surviving in the wilds—like a mechanical Tom Sawyer"

"That's wonderful," I said.

"It sure is," he said, almost teary eyed by now. "Oh how I love our weekend homestead."

We moved close to the fire and sat down on a chaise not too far from where Lara Whiddon was still reading the glossy. The fire was Tanya's doing—aesthetically pleasing, the flames themselves seeming to follow her directions to look pretty and colorful and evenly distributed, and they made the sound of a muttering baritone while the smoke twirled in whimsy up the chimney. Tanya seemed, at times, to be a sort of atmospheric magician and though I wouldn't say it out loud (for my friend was apparently suffering), I could understand how she'd drawn a following. Don disappeared for a minute and then came up from the basement and threw some hunks of old butcher block into the fire. "What's left of an old workbench in the basement," he said, delivering the little cubes of wood into the flames. "Came with the place. Been cutting it up all week. It's warped to hell."

When Tanya came into the living room from the kitchen, tray of fresh canapés poised upon her Barbie fingers, she stopped dead in her tracks. "Who the hell did *that*?" she said, glaring at the fire.

"It's the old workbench countertop from the basement," Don said again, his thick beard breaching before each word could leave.

"Well it looks like shit," she said, and put down the tray of canapés. "What a ridiculous looking fire," and she went to get the fireplace tongs.

"Probably maple is my guess," offered Don, finishing up his thought.

Tanya apparently couldn't stomach the aesthetic mismatch within the grid and was soon walking across the living room holding the fireplace tongs before her and within their jaws a flaming cube.

"Jesus Christ," Don said, following her toward the front door, "they're gonna burn up, honey. Don't make a scene. In ten minutes you won't even know the difference," to which Tanya replied by lunging toward her husband with the flaming cube. Of course the guests, we guests, were a little bemused and concerned, and then when the smoke detectors in the house started going off, we were annoyed. But at least the night had taken an interesting turn.

Using the screeching alarm to foil my shyness, I turned to Lara Whiddon and shouted, "This is a wonderful party."

"It certainly is," she shouted back. "Look at how much fun we're having."

"I love them both dearly," I shouted, "but I guess they've got some issues."

"I guess they have," she shouted back to me.

Then, after a brief pause, I shouted, "Alan," indicating self.

Mirroring my gesture, she shouted "Lara," but just then Don disabled the alarms, so her name broke into the silence and everyone turned. She blushed and went back to her reading.

Within a minute Tanya returned with the tongs poised for more action. We guests found ourselves counting the number of cubes still burning in the fireplace. Don was embarrassed at first, but after Tanya's second trip out the front door he poured himself a few fingers of Scotch and stood next to me.

"She's really lost it this time," he said. "I guess you can tell that we've been having our disagreements."

Through the window, illuminated by the house's flood lights, we could see her throwing the flaming cubes into the ice-crusted snow, a little plume rising up after each impact, as if a miniature spacecraft had just crashed. When she finished removing all the offending fuel from the fire, she returned to the tray of beige canapés and began passing them around. She did not look relaxed and she assiduously ignored her husband and me. Yet after twenty minutes she softened and even stroked the scruff on Don's neck during one pass. He got up and they walked outside together in conference.

I slid over on the chaise and invited Lara Whiddon to sit next to me. She accepted, and pretty soon we were chatting about the fight, the unseasonably warm winter, the East Village, where I live, and her hometown of Groton. Her eyes had dark half-moons under them, but the irises were clear and incisive, moving rapidly as she spoke and listened, as if she had been starved for conversation. Before long I told her I'd heard about her husband's death.

"Have you ever been in a bad marriage?" she said.

"No," I said. "I've never been married."

"It's something, I'll tell you. Trapped in a vault with a man who's become a stranger. So sad it has to happen. Jason was his name. Whip-smart but too easily swayed from . . ." and she drifted off.

"You?" I offered.

"Yes. He'd been seeing a number and *variety* of other people. Would you be a mensch and get me a glass of something red." I did as asked and returned.

"My husband," she continued, "he said he couldn't help it. We went to a therapist together and it was agreed that he was suffering from an addiction. A sex addiction."

"I don't suppose that comforted you," I said.

"It did nothing for me. I was addicted to him, after all. But it's okay," she added, "I'll be fine, believe me. I was raised to be as strong as an ox."

"And as graceful as a gazelle?" I offered, taking the chance and glancing at the rest of her.

"That's sweet of you. But in the wild a gazelle is a meat popsicle."

She looked at me but I had no reply.

"Well," she said, "this is exactly the tact I didn't want to take with a stranger. What else then? Do you have a cheerful topic handy?"

"Actually," I said, "did you hear about the robot in the woods?"

She looked shocked. "Well of course," she said. "It's the main reason I'm here—other than to see the happy couple."

"Oh. I beg your pardon. I didn't know anybody was taking it seriously."

"Absolutely seriously. Can you imagine a more thrilling story?"

I could, in fact.

"There seem to be rumors swirling around these parts like clouds in the sky," I said.

"There are rumors and there are verifiable events," she said, "and this is one of the latter. But I won't say anything more since you've made me feel like a bit of an idiot."

"Apologies," I said. "I didn't realize it was a sensitive issue."

"If you're around tomorrow maybe I'll tell you more. And I'm going to look for it, by the way, if you'd like to join me."

"I would," I said.

"Then tomorrow, after breakfast," and then I watched her raise her solid, graceful body and walk off in search of Tanya.

Guests were beginning to leave or move to their assigned sleeping locations—beds, sofas, spots on the floor. It was close to one in the morning but I stayed up for another hour, smoked a joint with Don out in the snow, and then was assigned one of the only places left, a spot on the floor next to Lara in a guest room on the first floor. Don gave me a foam sleeping mat and quilt. There was a third person in the room as well, a shadowy figure breathing evenly and silently at the far corner of the room. Soon I was on my back, my eyes adjusting to the dim room, which was lit by a sliver of moonlight coming in above one of the curtain rods. Within about twenty minutes I was beginning to drift off, and would have, if not for a strange sound that began to arise from the widow on the sofa beside me.

As silent as Lara had been during the party, she was obliged to carry out her mourning in her sleep where her ox-like upbringing had no relevance. In this state she seemed to be in an endless conversation, a kind of jet-powered whisper, a connubial lifetime of domestic exchanges compressed into these impossibly infinitesimal syllables that streamed out ceaselessly. Questions asked, questions answered, assertions, submissions, protests, retorts, laughter—all of it coming up without the bottleneck of consciousness or syntax to slow it down. Then, with a start and some wet, ugly gnashing, she woke up. I watched her through half-closed eyes. She sat bolt upright, looked around, remembered where she was, gave a long sigh and drifted back downward into the sofa. After that she wept. On it went, steady and raw, fluttering into the dark room like little bats.

While Lara was traveling her tragic road, I heard an argument that slowly, ghostlike, came to fill the house. I knew immediately it was Don and Tanya and that it was a reprise of the fire event. It was difficult to figure out exactly by what means the sound carried so well. It could have been through the vents (they had forced air heating) or somehow come down the chimney into the room's little fireplace and out to us. If I was right about the house, they were two floors above us. To my right, an incantation for the dead; above and around me, a marriage on the brink of collapse, the cause of which seemed to be a deeply mismatched aesthetic sensibility.

The next day Lara and I stuck around and joined Tanya and Don on a walk along the old Erie Lackawanna railroad tracks that follow the Delaware River. It was warm, in the fifties, and we could hear the snow melting all around us—in the river valley below and the granite cliffs above, a sound like milk in a giant bowl of cereal. Soon Lara and I had broken away from Don and Tanya, who were beginning to argue again. Don had been kicking at the snow and gravel between the railroad ties, not looking at his wife as she spoke. It didn't bode well. They moved off, south, toward the car, and we agreed to walk the mile or so back to their house after our search was completed.

"Now," Lara said, "this is what I've come to understand: A trio was up here from Queens in August. Up in Bryce's Eddy, about a mile north of here. You see there's a spot, I guess it's the eddy itself, where the river is very calm and clear. Well these kids were up there drinking beer and swimming. One of them kept diving deep, right down to the bottom of the river. And eventually he came up with this very unusual object." Here she paused and took a bite out a hummus and bean sprout sandwich that

Tanya had packed for her. At that moment I raised the flask of bourbon that Don had given me to my lips—hair of the dog. "The young man came up with an artificial foot. But not your ordinary prosthesis."

"I'm intrigued," I said. "Seriously," and she smiled. Her teeth were broad and healthy, white as the snow.

"This foot was intricately mechanical," she said.

"They're getting sophisticated these days. Lots of new recipients."

"Thing is, it's not clear what kind of artificial foot it was except, I think, a left one. It was very complex and, for example, there was no way of telling how it would have attached to a human leg. It was torn off from something bigger. The kids called the state police and now everyone's saying the authorities are looking for a robot."

"With a bad limp."

"Very funny, but correct. They can't really place the technology. It's beyond the most sophisticated prosthetics. When Tanya told me the story I didn't know what to say. It did something to me. A robot! And of course none of the city papers covered it. Only a couple of local papers up here—*The River Reporter*, the *Callicoon Democrat*, and one blog. But nothing's changed since the summer. No new leads."

Was it possible? I wondered, because she did seem completely serious and focused on this idea of a lost and maimed robot marooned in the winter forest, and the image began to appeal to me.

"It leaps out at you, doesn't it?" she said, seeing the expression on my face. "Not like those other rumors." But then I thought about the tragedy of her circumstances, the violence of her husband's death, the need to find a mission, a dramatic distraction to take her away from her own compartmentalized trauma.

I watched Lara bite into her sandwich again. I couldn't tell how much of this she was making up. She'd lost her husband and maybe, with him, a portion of her sanity. It was understandable. To be obsessed with finding an injured robot was somehow admirable, as if her mind had constructed the perfect therapeutic correlative to her situation. An emotionless "man" who was missing a piece of himself, a piece that could be reattached to make him whole again. If it did turn out she was truly and utterly mad, so be it. No harm could come from following her around for the day, just for the thrill of it. And she was becoming quite attractive to me, her pure emotional core exposed like it was. I'd never met anyone so lacking in pretension, so utterly stripped of falsity. We were alone on the tracks now, heading north. Below, islands of ice floated down the river. I looked back. Don and Tanya were two receding spots between the rails and were soon out of sight entirely.

Lara kept looking over into the drainage ditches on either side of the tracks. Here and there the snow had melted enough to expose muddy scrub and scattered trash.

"Are you really hoping to find the rest of the robot man?" I said, placing a hand around her elbow.

"It wouldn't have a gender, necessarily. But you never know," she said. "Really. It's not such an idiotic idea that some kind of experiment went haywire and the beta model escaped, fell down one of these hills, and lost a foot or more. I mean if it was only meant to function in a lab, then imagine what hitting some rocks could to it. It was probably a delicate thing."

She turned and faced me, her braids kicking around in the wind like sections of rope, and I saw nothing beyond her but the tracks vanishing into the curve of the valley, the granite cliffs looming above fringed with massive firs and spruces. We were hidden on the riverside by some tall, half-dead brush, but the entire valley seemed devoid of humanity anyway.

I took another deep swig from the flask because for an instant I thought I saw a glint up there on the cliffs. The bourbon was kicking in and I felt some heat welling up. Lara, with her loose jeans, her sturdy body, that mournful, saturated-with-sorrow bearing. Such beauty, sorrow, self-assurance and vulnerability. I wanted to fold her into me, kiss those tear-streaked cheeks and puffy eyes at the same time I wanted to make her come, just to give her some pleasure, some relief.

"Standing up," I said. "It's possible to do that without leaning on anything."

"Do what?"

"Make love. Screw. There's nobody around. You can be free with me. I'd like to give you some happiness, even if it's temporary."

"What?"

"Let's do it."

"Who *are* you?" she said.

I moved closer until our belt buckles collided. Clank. "I get like this sometimes. This—disinhibition. It's because I'm slightly, ever so slightly bi-polar," which was and is true.

She looked at me for some time, trying to decide if I was serious.

"This wasn't part of the plan," she said. " We are looking for a robot."

"But we are not robots," I said. "For example, I can go down on you," I said. "Get on my knees and suck you off. That's all about you, nothing about me. I think you can use this—as a gift, as therapy? Someone needs to give you something and expect nothing in return."

"Yes," she said, after looking around. "Do that."

"Say it," I said.

"Down," she said.

Looking her in the eyes—they were brown and flecked with shards of metallic blue as if she'd once been caught in a rain of jeweled shrapnel—I unwrapped her scarf and threw it down at her feet, in the snow and gravel, then I kneeled on it. I took off one of her boots, undid her pants, pulled them down along with her underwear until she could step out of them and then back into her boot. It took a minute or two to get the human machine warmed and accepting of me, but soon she was pushing forward into my mouth. Let her husband's memory fade into dust for these minutes, I thought. I put some snow in my mouth and let it melt in her. Slow, I thought, slow slow, but be precise and kind, brother, and make her husband spin. On it went, more snow, then, delicately, a thumb eased into her anus for the climax.

Still on my knees, I looked between her legs, down the tracks. In the distant distance a spot appeared. Silver, glimmering, it was too small and bright to be a train and moved too swiftly to be anything human. I dressed her as best as possible and then she pulled me up.

"Your turn," she said.

"That wasn't the intent."

"So what. Anything dangerous down there I should know about?"

"No."

"Then drop 'em."

She took me fully in her mouth, which was warm but the lips cold.

Over her beautiful bobbing head I saw a limping machine, getting into focus now. At first, from a distance, it appeared to be a man in a cheesy B-movie costume. On it came, looking more like a machine the closer it got. It was faceless and a small camera hung off to one side of its head, a broken bracket, loose wires, the lens cracked. Mud filled deep scratches and dents in its housing. Reeds stuck out in a few directions and in one of its hand-like things it cradled some kind of metallic disc. In place of one of its feet a folksy prosthesis made of a lump of driftwood and a small animal carcass, bones and all, were bound together with fishing line. Lara was skilled and pragmatic on her knees. I held onto her thick braids, pushed into her slightly as I approached my climax.

Afterward, she stood and we kissed hard and I held her tightly to me. I could taste myself in her mouth. Ten feet behind her the robot now stood still, its metallic arms still cradling what turned out to be an ancient Rambler hubcap. The machine was shedding drops of water, thawed ice from higher altitudes was my guess. Reeds and scraps of garbage that had become lodged in its mechanical joints blew about like hair as a gust of wind struck it. I buttoned my pants and cinched my belt. Then I looked over her shoulder one last time. "Your robot has arrived," I said, and she turned around.

★
★★
★ ★ ★
★ ★
★ ★
★★
★

There in the Delaware River, treading water thirty yards closer to the state of New York than the state of Pennsylvania, Rico, 19, saw a reflective object in the shadows below him. He dove down toward it. Down he went. Fifteen feet, twenty, deeper still. He held his hand out to the object and felt a smooth cleft as he lifted it from the riverbed. At first it was held fast by suction, but the river bottom, soft as pudding, soon gave it up. He rose toward the surface, holding it before him, a familiar shape, sunlight coming in through the water making it shimmer like a fish.

Marty and Dawn, watching from the rocky beach, had taken the opportunity of Rico's dive to fool around.

"I see something," their friend had said. "I'm going for it."

"Yeah yeah," Marty said, already getting excited at the prospect of thirty or forty seconds of uninterrupted groping with his girl. Dawn was wet from the midriff down and covered in goose bumps. The water was too cold and she had been too chicken to dive in. Marty couldn't wait to plant one on her, full throttle, and slip his hand under the elastic of her bikini. She was blonde and slim, tiny-breasted, thighs he'd never seen bare in broad daylight. And then Rico vanished into an expanding circle of golden water that seemed lighter at the center, where it churned.

It was a foot Rico returned to the surface with, an artificial, blindingly intricate one. It was trailing a few threads of river plants and still shedding silt from its endless hollows and seams.

"Holy shit," was how he announced his surfacing. He heard, through his water-filled ears, the snapping of elastic—*thwimp-imp*. Dawn, on shore, was straightening her bikini bottom. Marty, partially shielding himself, was glancing at his friend who was holding the artificial foot, ankle and all, above his head. With only one hand in the water, Rico treaded with difficulty.

"Holy shit," Marty said.

And then Dawn, "It's the most beautiful thing I've ever seen."